HEART'S Desire

BETH E. WESTCOTT

Scrivenings
PRESS
Quench your thirst for story.
www.ScriveningsPress.com

Published by Scrivenings Press LLC
15 Lucky Lane
Morrilton, Arkansas 72110
https://ScriveningsPress.com

Paperback ISBN 978-1-64917-092-7
eBook ISBN 978-1-64917-093-4

Library of Congress Control Number: 2020949285

Cover by Linda Fulkerson, www.bookmarketinggraphics.com

Published in association with Jim Hart of Hartline Literary Agency, Pittsburgh, PA.

To my husband, Frank, who supports me in my writer's journey and helps sell my books, and to my daughters, Heather and Alicia, and son, Clifford.

ACKNOWLEDGMENTS

God is good, and He provides. I'm grateful to have *Heart's Desire* published by Scrivenings Press with support and encouragement from Linda Fulkerson and Shannon Vannatter. To my family and friends who support me and pray for me, thank you. I'd also like to recognize the contribution of fellow authors and other members of the writing community who have been willing to share their knowledge and expertise with me to help me improve my writing and marketing skills.

*A*ubrey White searched the crowd of wedding guests seated on the groom's side. A young woman with black hair and an olive complexion, probably Jason's fiancée, sat with the Abbott family. But no Haleigh.

She shook her head.

Surely Haleigh's past friendship with the White family should win out over anger, hurt feelings, or whatever it was that made her avoid her friends for five years.

However, she wouldn't let Haleigh's non-appearance ruin this day. Today, her older brother, Mike, would marry Madison, the love of his life.

As Aubrey walked down the church aisle on her brother Willie's arm, dressed in a mid-calf length bridesmaid's gown of coral lace over crepe and white sandals, her gaze connected with Jeremy Abbott's dark brown eyes. He winked at her and smiled, igniting a spark of warmth that passed through her. She smiled back. Her cheeks grew hot, and she focused forward.

"You have an admirer, I see, Sis." Willie whispered in her ear.

Willie didn't miss much. "Mind your business," she whispered back.

He grinned. He'd probably been looking for Haleigh too. Not

long ago, Aubrey discovered that Willie's affection for their childhood friend ran deeper than friendship, even after five years.

Yesterday afternoon, Aubrey and her family had arrived in Rosemont, Madison's hometown, a four-hour trip from Greenlawn. After the rehearsal and dinner, they'd stayed in a motel.

Tears filled her eyes as Mike and Madison repeated their vows. The ceremony affirmed their love and commitment to each other and to God.

In the front row, her father sat with his arm around her mother. All their lives she and her brothers had a good marriage model before them: their parents.

Will I ever commit my life to one man, God? Will I ever be cherished as my mother is cherished by my father, and as Mike cherishes Madison?

Aubrey had kept her relationship with guys casual because she had other priorities, like finishing college and starting a career.

Jeremy was Haleigh's brother, Jason's identical twin, and a friend to Aubrey. His handsome face, firm jaw, brown eyes, and a wave of brown hair across his forehead, kept popping into her mind, making it hard to concentrate on the wedding service.

"Please join me in prayer."

The pastor's words jostled her mind back to the present. She hadn't missed much of the ceremony, had she? She bowed her head as he prayed for God's blessing on Mike and Madison. By the time the prayer ended, she'd turned her attention back to the happy couple as they kissed and stood before their guests as Mr. and Mrs. Michael White.

During the reception at the Rosemont Country Club, despite her best efforts to avoid doing it, Aubrey's eyes found Jeremy frequently. Occasionally she caught his gaze on her. Her stomach flip-flopped. She didn't understand her crazy reaction to her childhood friend.

Grandpa and Grandma White smiled at her from seats at

their table. Grandpa waved her over. He stood as she approached.

"Aubrey, we haven't talked to you since Christmas."

She kissed his cheek, the spicey scent of his aftershave triggering happy memories of sitting in his lap, listening to his stories. His eyes still twinkled with mischief.

"I know. It's been too long." She used the excuse that the busyness of school and work had replaced the time she used to spend with them.

"Did you have a good semester at school?" Grandma caressed her cheek.

"I did. My GPA is 3.9. I'm waiting now for my student teaching assignment for fall semester. Mom and Dad bought a car for me to use when I go back to school. If it's not too far, I'll live in the college dorm and drive back and forth each day."

"What are your plans after you graduate from Clark University?"

"I'm going to graduate school for my master's degree. My advisor gave me information about a couple of scholarships. If my student teacher evaluation is good enough, I may have my tuition fully covered the first year and half the second."

Grandpa grinned. "And I suppose one day we'll call you Dr. White, and you'll become a college president."

She smiled and shrugged. "That's the plan."

Someone stepped in beside her, and she breathed in the pleasant scent of a man's after shave. She took a step to the side and looked up into eyes like pools of chocolate. Again, her stomach flip-flopped, and her lips turned up on their own.

"Hello, Mr. and Mrs. White. It's good to see you." Jeremy's voice sent a shiver down her spine.

"Well, well." Grandpa White shook Jeremy's hand. His eyes shifted from Jeremy to Aubrey, and his lips twitched. "You're an Abbott—Jason or Jeremy?"

Aubrey knew the brothers well enough to tell the difference. Although they were identical in physical appearance, she saw subtle differences in body movements and facial expressions. Jason had a more competitive, out-going personality than Jeremy. Jeremy, the more sensitive twin, liked competition, but he didn't have to win.

Jeremy grinned. "I'm Jeremy, Mr. White. Jason is sitting over there with his fiancée, Carmella." He pointed across the room.

As she waited for Grandpa's response, Aubrey held her breath, imagining the wheels in her grandfather's head spinning. His humor was legendary.

"Fiancée, eh? It seems as though the marriage bug has bitten both our families." He looked directly at Jeremy, his lips twitching. "When are you getting hitched?"

"Huh!" Aubrey gasped. Heat rose in her face. Did Grandpa think she and Jeremy were ... had plans? Well, they did, but not together.

Jeremy opened his mouth, then closed it and licked his lips. Red crept up the back of his neck. "I'm working on it. These things take time, you know."

With a guffaw, Grandpa slapped Jeremy's arm. Grandma smiled and shook her head.

Aubrey pretended to smooth a wrinkle out of her dress. She didn't want Grandpa or Jeremy to get the idea she wanted to get married. Not to Jeremy. Not to any man. At least not for a long time.

Yet, she couldn't deny her attraction to this grown-up Jeremy in his dark blue, pinstriped suit, blue shirt, and blue-and-brown tie. He must be six feet tall now. She'd last seen Jeremy two years ago.

The old man chuckled and waved them away. "You young people go on. You don't want to waste all your time talking to us old people."

"It's not wasted time, Grandpa." Aubrey bent and kissed her grandfather's cheek, then her grandmother's. "I don't get to see you much anymore."

She avoided Jeremy's eyes as they turned away.

Had Aubrey's grandfather read his mind? During the wedding, and now at the reception, Jeremy could hardly take his eyes off her.

"Want to go for a walk, Aubrey?" He cleared his throat. "It's a beautiful day."

"You know, that sounds wonderful." She nodded and ran her fingers through her shiny blond hair that cascaded down her back but avoided looking directly at him. "I'm getting a little stiff from all the sitting."

As they moved toward the back door of the reception hall, Jeremy thought he detected a slight limp as she walked beside him. "Does your hip still bother you?"

Aubrey didn't respond. Had the question offended her? He opened the door and allowed her to precede him.

As soon as the door clicked shut behind them, she giggled.

"Aubrey?"

She walked a few more steps, turned toward him, and burst into laughter, then placed her fingers over her mouth, and the laughter diminished into giggles. "My grandfather gets away with saying such outrageous things." She laughed again. "I'm sorry, Jeremy. I hope he didn't embarrass you too much."

"No." Jeremy smiled.

Her blue eyes sparkled, and her golden hair glistened in the sun.

"Well, maybe a little," he confessed. "I only pointed out Jason and his fiancée."

"He probably would have found a way to tease, no matter what you said. You know my brothers come by their sense of humor genetically, especially Jesse."

"I know." Jeremy chuckled.

A rose garden lay before them, with smooth stone walkways and white benches. A gazebo stood across the lawn, at the other end of a stone path. When Jeremy indicated that direction with his hand, Aubrey looped her arm through his. His breath caught, and a surge of pleasure passed through him at her touch.

"These stones might be a little rough for walking in heels." She raised one sandal-clad foot.

He remembered her as independent and competitive, so her request for assistance surprised him.

For many years, he'd thought of Aubrey as another sister, just as Haleigh thought of Aubrey's brothers as hers. They still texted or messaged occasionally, and he and his brother sent her a card for her birthday every year.

The attraction he felt for her now had sparked when their eyes met as Aubrey walked down the aisle at the church.

"I'm sorry, I didn't answer your question. Grandpa set me off." She giggled again. "I don't have a lot of trouble with my hip, but I have to stay active. Sometimes, when I sit for long periods, it gets stiff."

"It must be hard sitting for classes at college."

"Not usually. Walking between classes and being on the track team keep me limber."

"You don't play basketball anymore?" An athlete himself, he'd admired her athletic skill in high school. He understood her grief after the accident, when her friend Leanna Nelson died and she lost the hope of a scholarship for college.

She shook her head. "No. I gave that up, although the doctor said I could try playing again during my senior year. I enjoyed basketball, but it wasn't my whole life." She took a deep breath. "It wasn't as much fun without Leanna. Being on the university track team helps me stay in shape and be competitive. How about you? Are you still playing sports?"

"I played soccer in the fall and did track in the spring during college. I tried to concentrate on my studies. Now that I'm going to graduate school, my sporting days are over, although I want to keep in shape."

"I heard both you and Jason had been accepted at seminary. Are you planning to be a pastor?"

"I feel the Lord's calling me to preach and be a pastor, and seminary will give me good preparation."

"My roommate, Christina, dated a seminary student for a while. He was a nice guy."

Jeremy tipped his head. "Does going to seminary make me a nice guy too?"

"You're a nice guy anyway." Her eyes met his as she blushed and bit her lip.

Loving her response, given without hesitation, he swiped his hand across his mouth, but the grin remained.

As he leaned toward her ear, a soft, sweet, peach fragrance invaded his senses. He patted her hand. "I like you too, Goldie." He used his childhood name for her.

Her lips turned up at the corners.

"By the way, you look quite lovely today." Aubrey had always been a pretty girl, and she'd become a beautiful young woman.

She stole a quick glance at him and murmured, "Thank you, Jeremy."

They stopped with the gazebo before them.

"Do you want to sit here for a while?" He wasn't quite ready to relinquish her back to the wedding crowd.

"Maybe we'd better return to the reception. Grandpa might get more ideas."

"Would it really bother you if he did?"

She peered at him then shook her head. "No, I don't think so." She raised her chin. "I think I'm tough enough to take his teasing. I've had years of practice."

"That's for sure."

As the only girl in the family with three brothers, she'd learned to stand up for herself.

Several other wedding guests, including Jason and Carmella, exited and stood on the stone patio. Children ran around in the grass. A small group of older adults stood by the door.

"Jason's fiancée is very nice." Aubrey waved to the couple. "I think she and Jason will be happy." Laying her free hand on his arm, she stopped him. "I wonder how you feel about your twin being married."

He inhaled her peach fragrance as her nearness and direct gaze jumbled his thoughts. A coherent response escaped him until he lowered his eyes and rearranged his thoughts.

"At first, I was jealous. Jason is my best friend as well as my twin. But Jason is happy, and Carmella is good for him. I think I can honestly say I'm glad for them. He's going to a different seminary than me, and I think it will be harder having him so far away than having him married."

With his twin planning to marry in August, Jeremy sometimes felt as though he was losing his best friend. In his heart, though, he knew he'd never lose his brother. As adults, their relationship had already undergone changes that weren't unexpected or totally unwelcomed.

The door of the reception hall opened. Aubrey gestured with her hand. "Look, Mike and Madison are coming out for a photo shoot." The photographer followed the newlyweds.

Jeremy and Aubrey stopped, standing a little to the side and behind the photographer. Aubrey withdrew her hand from his arm, her attention on her brother and his wife.

"The rose garden is a perfect background for wedding photos. The photographer took pictures of the wedding party and families at the church. I wonder why they didn't plan to take at least some of them here." She rubbed her hip where a pocket might be located. "I wish I had my phone with me, to take some pictures."

He pulled his cell phone out of his pocket and snapped pictures of the bride and groom, then turned and focused on Jason and Carmella. They smiled when they saw him and posed with their arms around each other.

The photographer's camera whirred. Mike and Madison kissed.

What would it be like to kiss Aubrey? Better not go there. He wanted to reserve his kisses for the woman he married.

He swung his phone to focus on his companion. "Aubrey." He captured her sparkling eyes and beautiful smile when she looked his way. Then he snapped a picture of the two of them side-by-side. He wanted to hold on to this moment.

"I'll send you my photos."

"Thanks." She brushed wisps of hair back from her temple with her fingertips. "I'm glad you came today. I miss the times the Abbotts and Whites spent together when you lived in Greenlawn. I'm sorry that Haleigh didn't come."

"Me too." Jeremy pocketed his phone and looked toward his brother. "It doesn't seem right that an Abbott should miss a White event, or vice versa. But she had her excuses, something to do with her dog. We tried our best, but you know Haleigh's stubborn streak."

"I do, but this one has been particularly long."

Jeremy worried about his sister. He and Jason had laughed with her, teased her, protected her, and picked on her and her friends as big brothers were expected to do. They'd always been a close-knit family. Underneath a happy exterior, Haleigh had encased her wound in a box, and she refused to allow it to heal. At least that's how Jeremy saw it.

The laughter and screams of the children drew his attention. The girls in dresses and the boys in dress pants, shirts, and ties played tag. Some of the watchful adults cautioned them to be careful.

He turned his attention back to Aubrey. "What are you doing this summer?"

"I'm working at the Hillside Diner in Greenlawn. I would have worked today, but Mr. Duncan knew it was my brother's wedding and made sure I had the entire weekend off. How about you—do you have a summer job?"

"I'm an intern at our church in Wellsburg. The church has a scholarship fund, and Jase and I are both benefitting from it. Plus, they're paying me to work this summer."

Aubrey gazed at him, her blue eyes framed by dark lashes. He broke eye contact and brushed hair off his forehead.

"I'm working with the kids: VBS, Kids' Club, field trips, things like that. Even in our small town, a lot of kids don't attend church. Many of them live in troubled homes. We want to provide support for them and a safe place where they can have fun and learn about Jesus."

When the playing children screamed with laughter, both he and Aubrey turned their heads. The children's game evoked memories of the childhood games he used to play.

"It's been a while since I played tag." Aubrey looked at him. "I wanted to go to Haiti with a missions team from Clark, but when Mike planned his wedding, I couldn't go. Maybe next year. I have to make some money this summer if I want to finish my senior year without borrowing more."

"The seminary recommends short-term missions experience for its pastoral students, so I'll probably go somewhere within the next couple of years." How much more interesting a trip like that might be if Aubrey went as well.

Whoa! His imagination galloped far ahead of reality. He wanted to give his best to preparing for his calling without distractions. He had two years of seminary to complete before committing himself to a serious relationship. Unlike his twin, he planned to wait.

"Will you be working during the school year?"

"When I'm on campus I will."

He detected faint freckles crossing the bridge of her nose. "What do you mean?"

"I'll be student teaching for the fall semester. So, depending on where I'm assigned, I probably won't have much time. During the spring semester I'll be working in the admissions office for the university. I've been doing that for several semesters, on work-study."

As she talked, he watched her face, memorizing the details:

her blue eyes with dark lashes, the shape of her nose, the curve of her cheek, her full lips.

Was it Mike's wedding, or Jason's engagement, or God nudging him to think of a future with her? Today, for the first time, he saw his childhood friend with new eyes.

He didn't want to move too fast into a relationship, but it wouldn't hurt to talk on the phone, text, or email occasionally as friends. They'd done that since the Abbotts moved away from Greenlawn anyway.

"Goldie, let's keep in touch this summer."

"I'd like that." Her smile sent another spark through him. "We're friends on Facebook, and you have my phone number. And I have yours."

"That will be great! And I already know where you live."

What a day!

Aubrey ran the back of her hand across her damp forehead and took a deep breath. The hot, sticky air outdoors made her thankful for air conditioning inside.

Every day the restaurant became busier, which meant more money from tips, but an exhausting routine as well.

As hostess, with a waitress who'd called in sick, she'd rushed around since coming in. A few times she helped the busboy clear off the tables, which filled almost as soon as they emptied.

A sea of faces formed a line of waiting diners. "A table for four?" Removing four menus from the pocket at the end of the counter, she led them, a couple, an older woman, and a young man, to a table by a window and laid down the menus.

"Well, well, imagine meeting Aubrey White waitressing in a restaurant." The familiar, mocking voice from the past caught her attention.

Startled, she looked up into the blue eyes and smirking mouth of Derek Hall. Her stomach took a dive.

"Derek." His father's voice held a warning.

Derek pulled out a chair and sat. He'd been a star football player for Greenlawn High. Talented and popular, he frequently pushed the buttons between acceptable and unacceptable behavior, and his teasing often bordered on bullying. As Leanna's friend, Aubrey became better acquainted with him than she would've otherwise.

Back then, he'd had a crush on her, but she refused to join his admiration society. She'd stood up to Derek, but girls like Haleigh Abbott often became a target of his bullying.

He'd been behind the wheel, DWI, the night Leanna died.

The last time she'd seen him was in court, where he'd been sentenced to four years in prison, followed by parole and community service for a drunk driving fatality. He didn't want to take responsibility for his action, trying to lay the blame on the girls for getting into the car with him.

"Uh—hello, Derek. I've worked here every summer since I graduated from high school." G-r-r-r. She didn't have to explain herself to him. Derek's arrogant attitude angered her now as much as it did back then.

She turned to the three older adults. Derek's mother and grandmother fixed their eyes on their menus. Only his father met her eyes briefly.

"I'll be with you to take your orders in a few minutes." She escaped as quickly as she could without being rude and blew a tendril of hair back from her face. Her hands shook as she stopped to pick up a heavy tray of dirty dishes to carry to the kitchen.

A few steps inside the door from the dining room, she suddenly crashed to the floor on her knees. Dishes and food scraps flew. She turned from the kneeling position to sit on the floor.

A sharp pain in her right leg drew her eyes to a long gash in her pant leg, just below her knee. The fabric darkened and red oozed out. She bit her lip to keep from crying. She must have fallen on a piece of broken glass.

Someone handed her a bunch of napkins, which she pressed against the cut. Embarrassed by her fall, the food stains on her white blouse, and the chaos that erupted around her, she pushed her palms against the floor to get her feet under her.

"Wait, Aubrey!" Mr. Duncan, the restaurant owner, appeared and assessed the situation. "Okay, let's get this mess cleaned up!" He probed her leg gently with his fingers before he helped her stand. "I don't think anything's broken. Go to the break room, sit down, and relax. I'll get the first aid kit and be with you in a minute."

The busboy and a couple of waitresses brought a broom and mop and began clean-up.

Aubrey took a deep, shaky breath and limped away. Dropping into a chair and stretching her leg in front of her, she rolled up her pant leg. With a napkin she wiped at the blood that formed rivulets down to her ankle, then pressed several napkins against the cut. She tried to still her trembling with three deep, cleansing breaths.

"Good job, kids." Mr. Duncan spoke from the open door of the employee break room. "Better get back to work. There are hungry people out there." Her boss turned toward her. "Now, Aubrey, let's look at you." He dragged out a chair and sat facing her, sliding his hands into latex gloves.

She bit her lip as he cleansed the cut and checked for glass embedded in the wound.

"How did this happen?" He pressed a gauze pad against it.

"I'm not sure, Mr. Duncan." Aubrey shook her head. Tears stung her eyes, but she refused to give in to them. "It happened so fast. I'm sorry." She watched him place several clean gauze pads and tape over the cut. "Is someone taking the order from my table?" As busy as they were, she didn't want to give Derek an excuse to cause a scene.

"Yes." His calmness calmed her. "I think you're going to need stitches. Is there someone in your family available to take you to Urgent Care?"

"My mother should be home." She pulled her phone from her pocket, then moaned. "Oh, no, my phone is smashed!"

"I've got it." He had his phone already in hand.

AUBREY LAY BACK on the living room sofa, propped up by pillows, with a row of neat stitches below her knee. It throbbed. She moaned. "I can't work, I can't go anywhere, and my phone is broken."

Complaining didn't help. She could use her laptop to message, but it sat on her desk upstairs in her room. Her mother had left to get her pain medication and antibiotic at the pharmacy.

If she didn't work, she didn't get paid. Mr. Duncan insisted she stay home tomorrow, echoing the doctor's orders: give her leg a day of rest. An x-ray had revealed no other damage from her fall. This was simply an annoyance. She'd been through much worse.

Winning the girls' basketball championship her sophomore year in high school had been exhilarating. Aubrey and Leanna had both played well, but Leanna scored the most points for the team, even though she was only a sophomore. Everyone knew Leanna would win a sports scholarship for college and become a basketball star.

"Derek has his car, and he wants to take us for a victory ride. Come on, Aubrey." Leanna pulled on her arm.

"No, let's wait for the team victory ride around town on the school bus. That's a tradition for championship teams."

"Aw, come on, Aubrey. We'll be back in time for that."

Three days later, Aubrey woke up in the hospital with a broken hip and other injuries. Her world had changed forever. She should have died, not Leanna. Since her friend hadn't believed in Jesus, she hadn't been ready to die.

When she heard the back door close, Aubrey wiped tears from her eyes.

Mom walked into the living room with a pharmacy bag and a

bottle of water and handed them to Aubrey. "The instructions are on the bottles in the bag."

"Thanks, Mom." She pulled out two pill bottles.

"How are you doing?" Mom, the most caring person she knew, laid a small pillow under her knee.

"Other than the pain and the fact I can't work, I'm fine." She regretted the sarcasm in her voice. "I'm sorry, Mom. It's not your fault I'm lying here."

"Apology accepted. Is there anything else you need?'

"My laptop and book are on my desk upstairs. Will you get them for me?"

She swallowed her pills while Mom went upstairs.

After messaging her sister-in-law, her friend Christina, and a few other people, she read for a while. Drowsiness overcame her, and she slept for a couple of hours before supper.

That evening, her brothers went to Willie's building site, to build shelves for his florist shop. Her parents sat in the living room to watch the news and read.

Positioning herself comfortably on the sofa, Aubrey opened her laptop to look up the websites her advisor had told her about, with information about scholarships.

A scholarship would mean less money she'd have to borrow and pay back.

AUBREY AWOKE to the sound of footsteps in the hallway and on the stairs, and to the smell of coffee.

On a normal day, she would be joining her family in their morning ritual. She flipped back her covers and sat up. Moaning in the process, she swung her legs over the side of her bed. All five feet, eight inches of her body ached from her fall yesterday. The stitches made a line several inches long below her right kneecap, the area bruised and tender.

The front door closed, and her father's car started. Probably her brothers were finished in the bathroom by now. Time for her to get up.

She pushed to her feet, slowly shifting weight to her right leg. It supported her. Some of the stiffness drained off as she shuffled to the bathroom.

This morning's Bible reading from the book of James focused on patience, aka endurance or perseverance. Her own present trial, her wounded knee, was nothing compared to the persecution the early Christians suffered. They lost their jobs, their property, and even their lives by taking a stand for Christ.

Good grades, popularity, and success had always been easy for her. The only exception had been the long months in the hospital, rehab, and physical therapy after the accident. Then she'd endured physical pain and mental anguish because of her own poor choices.

Patience had a lot to do with faith, believing God and trusting Him to bring her through the challenges she faced. She didn't think she interfered with Him by using the physical and mental abilities with which He'd gifted her.

Praying for patience came hard. She had to admit her own weakness.

After dressing in khaki shorts and a light blue knit top, she braided her hair in a single plait down her back and made her bed. Everything took a little longer to accomplish this morning.

Holding the bannister firmly, she walked down the stairs, then limped into the kitchen, and collapsed into a chair.

Her mother looked up from writing on a piece of paper, the grocery store circular spread beside her. "Are you okay?" Her gaze searched Aubrey's face, then traveled to her knee and back. "Are you hungry?"

She nodded. "I am and I am." Normally she would serve herself. Instead, she propped her right leg on another chair. "Just some oatmeal and a banana, please." She shook her head. "I did a really stupid thing yesterday. It was embarrassing. Even though I need the money, I'm not sure I could face everybody today." She sighed. "I feel so … useless."

"You'll be fine. The doctor said to just watch for infection." Mom set a bowl, a spoon, and a banana in front of Aubrey. She spooned steaming oatmeal into the bowl and took a carton of milk from the refrigerator.

"Would you like some tea?"

"Yes, please."

Mom placed a tea bag in a cup and poured in hot water. "Mr. Duncan called to assure us that the restaurant's insurance will take care of any expenses from your accident. He seemed really concerned." She set the cup in front of Aubrey.

"Thanks, Mom." She inhaled the tea's warm fragrance as she stirred in sugar and added a little milk. "Mr. Duncan is a super boss. He treats his employees and customers well. I think that's why his restaurant business is so successful."

Her mother left for a meeting at church and a trip to the grocery store.

After eating her breakfast, Aubrey placed her dishes in the dishwasher and grabbed a bottle of water from the refrigerator. The stitches pulled as she limped into the living room. Her leg hurt, but she'd do without pain medication if she could.

The stillness shouted at her. What could she do? Her new phone should arrive tomorrow so she could contact friends and find out what was happening in the world. Her book and laptop lay upstairs on her desk because her focus this morning had been getting down the stairs. Climbing up the stairs right now was not an option.

Oh, for the days when she took the stairs up two at a time and jumped down three stairs from the bottom.

She grabbed the TV remote and flipped through the channels. Nothing interesting on.

The family photo albums on the bookcase caught her attention. Although Mom had photographs stored on flash drives, she chose to keep photo albums she could hold and show visitors.

Aubrey pulled them from the shelf, stacked them in her arms, and made her way to the sofa. With a groan she sat, propped her sore knee on a small pillow, and leaned back against some larger cushions. Getting herself into a comfortable position, she laid back her head, totally bored.

"How could you be so clumsy, Aubrey?" A day off had not been her plan for today.

Mr. Duncan needed her at work, and she needed the money. Why had she let Derek's presence shake her up? She should have watched where she stepped.

Purple, black, and blue bruises surrounded the tiny stitches below her kneecap, the area swollen and tender. The pain had eased a bit without medication.

The family calico cat, Sweetie Pie, glided into the room with a brief "mew," and invited herself to join Aubrey on the couch. The cat sniffed the scrapbooks and stared at her.

"Silly old cat." Aubrey rubbed her hand across the cat's soft fur and scratched behind her ears. Sweetie Pie began to purr. She'd been a kitten the year of Aubrey's accident and had kept her company through many lonely hours.

The Whites had a couple of dogs during Aubrey's growing-up years. Willie had suggested a pot-bellied pig when he was in middle school, but Mom said an emphatic no. The cat was their only pet now. Sweetie Pie curled up against Aubrey's side and went to sleep.

Aubrey opened the album numbered one. Her parents smiled back at her from photos of their wedding and their early life together. As she turned the pages, each of the children appeared in the family circle in order of birth: Mike, then her, Willie, and last Jesse.

Would she marry, or would she remain single and focused on her career? She imagined herself in a wedding photo with Jeremy as the groom. Marriage, if she ever married, was still in the future for her. She closed the first album and pushed the thoughts away.

The second album included many photos of the Three Sisters: at summer camp, at the mall, being silly together, playing games with their brothers, always smiling. So many memories they'd made together when they were kids.

Only a few photos of the threesome were in the third album. Most of the photos here had been taken during Aubrey's later teen years, not so long ago: she and her brothers in their sports uniforms, Willie in his gardens, she and Leanna playing basketball.

Aubrey leafed slowly through the pages with pictures after the accident: in the hospital, in rehab, and therapy.

The photos reminded her of the loneliness and pain as she recovered, mourned Leanna's death, and struggled to overcome survivor's guilt. By this time, her best-friend relationship with Haleigh Abbott and Katie Mann had ended. Though the physical and emotional strain of the accident and therapy took its toll, she healed.

Aubrey rubbed at the ghost pain in her left hip and repositioned the pillow under her right knee. Renewed throbbing in her knee and the ache in her body convinced her that she needed to take the overdue medication.

The cat looked up at her reproachfully for disturbing her and went back to sleep.

The next photos took her back to the White family vacation at Yellowstone National Park, and another vacation while hiking a part of the Appalachian Trail, her high school graduation and Willie's, and Jesse goofing around in his cap and gown. She yawned as she closed the album and checked her watch. Mom should be home any time.

The fourth album contained recent pictures, and she knew her mother would soon be adding Mike's wedding photos. Aubrey relaxed against the pillows and closed her eyes. What could she do next?

Her eyes popped open. The fog cleared from her mind. How long had she been asleep?

The last album lay on her stomach. She dropped it to the floor on top of the other three and shifted to a more comfortable position. Sweetie Pie protested, jumped off the couch, and stalked out of the room.

Her mom opened the front door. "Come in."

"Hello, Mrs. White." A familiar male voice rumbled.

A chill passed down her spine.

Footsteps in the hallway. Mom entered the living room. "Are you ready for some company, Aubrey?"

3

"*How's* the knee, Goldie?" Jeremy Abbott grinned at her over Mom's shoulder.

She smiled back. He and Jason had nicknamed the Three Sisters Goldie, Red, and Beanie. He had called her Goldie at Mike's wedding. Except for Jeremy, no one had called her that since the Abbotts moved away five years ago.

Butterflies activated in her stomach. "Jeremy? How ...? What are you doing here?" She sat up.

"Well, that's a nice welcome. I came all this way to see you because I heard you got hurt, and that's the greeting I get?" He sounded indignant, and he placed one hand on his hip, but the corners of his mouth twitched.

"I didn't mean it that way." She pulled her braid across her shoulder. "It's just that I didn't expect you. Why ... how did you get here so soon?"

"Mom messaging. You know, your mom called my mom."

Mom left the room with a smile on her face.

"I stopped to get this for you. If there were blue roses, I would've bought one." He stepped close and handed her a white bud vase containing a pink rose with baby's breath and a fern

23

stem. "Your brother will have quite a place when he gets finished."

"I know." She detected the pleasant scent of his after shave. "I'm proud of Willie. He's worked hard." She buried her nose in the rose. "Thank you. This is pretty." Holding the vase and hoping not to spill the water, she attempted to turn to face him.

"Here, let me help you." Jeremy took the vase from Aubrey's hand and placed it on the end table beside her.

His fingers brushed hers. Her fingers tingled.

He pushed over the hassock and placed the pillow under her knee. His touch sent electricity through her.

Heat rose in Aubrey's face with Jeremy's eyes focused on her bare legs. The shorts had been her choice this morning because they didn't rub against her injury. Now she wished she'd worn her jean skirt, which came to just below her knees.

Red crept up his neck and into his cheeks. He backed away quickly.

"Thank you." She licked her lips. Her leg still tingled from his touch, as she tried to relax and ignore the new sensations the grown-up version of her old friend stirred in her.

"So, what happened?" He sat in a chair across from her and placed one knee over the other.

"I fell at work and cut my knee. But I guess you know that already."

"Looks like quite a bruise as well." He nodded and gestured toward her knee with his hand. "Did you trip on something, or did someone knock you down?"

She leaned forward to shift the pillow under her knee. "I'm not sure. We were extremely busy, and I was rushing around. No one pushed me." She shoved back the memory of Derek Hall's mocking face and words, refusing to give Derek credit for this accident.

"One second I carried a tray of dirty dishes, and the next I hit the floor. I'm not usually that clumsy. My knee landed on broken glass. So here I am, on the couch with stitches and unable to work." She grabbed another throw pillow and hugged it. She had to stop whining.

JEREMY BIT his lip to keep from smiling at the frustration in her voice. Aubrey didn't like to have her plans interrupted.

"That's why I'm here, to cheer you up. Here's a card from my family." He stood and stepped forward.

"Didn't you have to work today?" She took the blue envelope he held out. "You said in your last email you had Vacation Bible School next week." She read the card with a smile and slid it back into the envelope.

"VBS is next week. About a hundred kids have pre-registered. It's mostly organized, but I brought my laptop so I can do a little work." He stretched his legs in front of him. "I had an interview with my advisor at seminary this morning. And since that's closer to Greenlawn than Wellsburg is, I thought I'd visit. I like coming back to Greenlawn and don't get much opportunity to do it."

"It's nice to see you. My phone got smashed when I fell, and I forgot to bring my laptop downstairs, so I've been out of communication with the world. I didn't know how much I depended on the phone. I'm glad you came."

His heart warmed at her welcoming words. "I'm thankful your injury wasn't more serious. Not like the other time."

"Right. I've had a few moments of déjà vu since yesterday. But this time it's just a few stitches and a day out of work without weeks of pain and therapy."

"Are you kids ready for some lunch?" Mrs. White spoke from the kitchen doorway.

"Sure am." Jeremy broke his gaze with Aubrey and looked at her mother. "I had breakfast rather early this morning."

"Is it lunchtime already?" Aubrey peered at her watch. "I guess I slept the morning away, didn't I? If you'll excuse me, I'll be right back." She swung her legs to the floor and pushed herself up, then straightened her right knee as she put weight on it.

Although tempted to do so, Jeremy didn't offer to help her stand. "I'll be here. Wouldn't want to miss lunch."

She favored her knee as she crossed the room and headed down the hall to the bathroom. He joined Mrs. White in the kitchen, where she set out cold cuts and cheese.

"Aubrey never did like being told she couldn't do something, but I'm glad the doctor and Mr. Duncan told her to stay home today." She pulled a tray of ice cubes from the refrigerator freezer. "He's a thoughtful boss. She likes working for him."

"That's good." He paused with his hand on the back of a chair. "Thank you for letting me come, Mrs. White. It's a little easier to be able to stop here before going back to Wellsburg."

She handed him the tray of ice cubes, and he placed several in each glass.

"I don't get back here often enough." He refilled the tray with water and returned it to the freezer.

"You know you're welcome any time. I'm sure Aubrey's glad for your company. It's quiet here during the day." She looked the table over. "I think everything's ready."

Aubrey entered the kitchen. "Mom, did you know Jeremy was coming?" She put her hand against the doorway and counter as she made her way to the chair Jeremy pulled out for her. "Thank you."

"Yes, Aubrey." Her mother smiled and nodded. "He called and asked if it would be all right."

"And you didn't warn me? Mom!"

"If you remember, we had some excitement here yesterday. I planned to tell you, but it slipped my mind."

"Don't you like surprises, Aubrey?" Jeremy sat in the chair across from her.

She shook her head "No." Then she looked at him and tilted her head. "Yeah, I guess they're okay sometimes."

The softness in her blue eyes nearly took his breath away.

Mrs. White didn't indicate she noticed. She asked Jeremy to give thanks for the food, and they began to eat.

Having lunch with Aubrey and her mother was a lot more fun than eating alone in a fast-food restaurant. He tried to keep his mind on their conversation. Everything about this young woman interested him. She was the same person he'd known all his life, so what sparked his interest in her now?

If he didn't have two years of seminary ahead, and she didn't have at least two additional years of school for her masters' degree, he'd like to court her and see where it led.

When they finished eating, Jeremy collected their dishes from the table and placed them in the dishwasher.

"You didn't have to do that, Jeremy, but thank you anyway." Aubrey's mother busied herself with putting away the remaining food.

"I don't mind. My mother expects Jason and me to help out at home."

"Your mother has taught you well. I expect my boys to help in the kitchen."

A smile played on Aubrey's lips. "You and Mrs. Abbott always said men should know how to cook, clean the house, and mend clothes because they might have to do it for themselves one day."

"Yes, Elizabeth and I share a lot of like ideas."

A girls' day out when they were kids had meant that Jeremy, Jason, and Aubrey's brothers had been left in charge of meal preparation and clean-up while Aubrey and Haleigh, and maybe Katie, went shopping or to a church event with their mothers.

He closed the dishwasher and faced Aubrey. A walk would be easy exercise for her, and knowing her as he did, she needed something to do. And besides, he wanted to see the neighborhood and the house where he'd lived.

"Do you feel up to a walk?"

"I think I'd like that, although I may not be able to go far. I'm going stir crazy." She rose from her chair.

"I could carry you...on my back. Like when we were kids."

Mrs. White pushed out her cheek with her tongue, and Aubrey blushed.

"Just teasing." The heat rose in his face again. Her curves reminded him they were kids no longer. "Let's go for that walk."

As Aubrey made her way to the front door, she used the wall to keep her balance. He followed, pulled the door shut behind them, and bumped into her when she stopped abruptly at the top of the steps.

"I'm sorry." He stepped to her side. "Are you in pain?"

"I actually feel better when I move." She grimaced as she held the top of the railing. "It's the steps."

He offered her his arm, and she looped her arm through it. The sensation of her soft skin on his arm sent a shock wave through him, and his muscles tensed. His heart thudded.

"Thanks. This is much easier."

"Glad to help." That she was willing to accept his help doubled the pleasure.

The shade of the trees along the sidewalk gave relief from the heat of the sun as they strolled. Sunglasses shielded their eyes from the glare, but Jeremy regretted he couldn't see her blue eyes. Her long blond hair, pulled back into a braid, gave off the scent of peaches.

Aubrey sighed. "I hope I can go back to work tomorrow. Hillside is so busy right now, Mr. Duncan suggested I might try for a few hours. The cut looks clean and is healing, so I want to go."

"I guess you're ready to get back into action, but maybe you shouldn't carry any heavy trays." Jeremy tried to gauge her comfort. "We don't want you to fall again."

"I know. Mr. Duncan said I can sit behind the cash register." She slowed her pace.

"Your mother said I'm welcome to stay overnight." He

shortened his stride when her steps lagged. "I have to leave early tomorrow morning."

"Good." She paused and looked up at him. "I mean, good that you can stay."

He raised his eyebrows. "I'm glad you clarified that. I thought maybe you didn't want me here."

She smiled and looked away. Did that mean she did or didn't want him to stay? Aubrey followed his lead without resisting when Jeremy directed their steps toward the Abbott's former home around the block.

The neighborhood where he'd lived for his first seventeen years brought a rush of memories. "I always feel like I'm coming home whenever I return to Greenlawn." Jeremy waved to a neighbor in his yard.

"I'm sorry we can't do something more active. Remember the hikes the youth group used to take to the fire tower? I'd love to be able to do that today. I feel useless just sitting around,"

"You're not sitting around. We're taking a walk." A dog barked at them from the window of a house. "I don't think I'll ever move back to Greenlawn to live, but I'll always look forward to visiting." Especially if Aubrey was here.

"Greenlawn has always been home to me, but I'm not planning to live here forever." Her shaded eyes turned his way. "I don't expect to apply for a teaching position here or live here after graduation, although my family is still here. After I get my doctorate, it'll be time for me to see the world. I'm looking forward to seeing where God takes me."

Would he and Aubrey see the world together? His heart galloped with *what if* while his mind said, *Whoa!*

They paused in front of Jeremy's former home.

"Look, they've kept up Gram's flower beds." Some of the flowers looked the same. "I'm glad. And they still have a swing in the apple tree." He breathed in the scent of newly mown grass. "I wonder if they've made any changes inside. I wish I could go in and look around."

"I come by here from time to time just to look at the flowers and remember." Aubrey let go of his arm and grasped the fence, leaving his arm empty and cold. "Haleigh, Katie, and I spent many hours on the swing. I've met the family who lives here, but I don't know them well." She leaned against the fence. "I don't think I can make it much farther, Jeremy."

He flexed his biceps. "Remember, I can take you on my back."

"You goof." She laughed, her cheeks turning pink. "I don't think so. I'm not sure you could do it now anyway, with my bum knee."

They sauntered on around the block in the direction of Aubrey's house, her hand resting in his elbow.

"We had a lot of fun when we were kids."

"Yeah." He looked over his shoulder at his childhood home. "Lots of great memories."

The walk back didn't last long enough.

"There's shade in the back yard, Jeremy, Let's go there instead of going inside."

"Good idea." He liked Aubrey's mother, but he preferred private time with Aubrey.

They headed around the side of the house.

"I think I'm walking into a page from *Better Homes and Gardens*!" He stopped and whistled. "Is all this Willie's work?" Before him lay a beautifully landscaped yard of flowers, shrubs, and a vegetable garden. "My grandmother would love to see this."

"Yes, isn't it beautiful? Willie adds something every year. He needs his own place."

Mindful of her wounded leg, he helped her settle comfortably in the chaise lounge in the shade of the sugar maple near the patio. He lowered himself to the cool grass, where he could be close to Aubrey.

"Are you coming to Jason's wedding next month?" He pulled a blade of grass and placed it between his front teeth, appreciating the coolness of the shade and the grass under him as he leaned back on his elbows.

She removed her sunglasses and laid them in her lap. He tucked his into his shirt pocket.

"I've asked for the time off, but since I'd have to take more than one day, I doubt I'll get it. A lot of others have requested that weekend."

"Oh." He threw the piece of grass on the ground and tried to mask his disappointment. "I'd hoped to see you again this summer. You'll be missed, you know."

Her blue eyes met his gaze. He could hardly breathe.

"I'll miss being there." She pulled her braid over her shoulder and looked away. "My parents plan to go, and probably Willie and Jesse."

"School will start a couple of weeks after the wedding." He sat up. "I was impressed with the seminary grounds at Clark. I'm glad I chose to attend there, although it will be strange not to have Jason there too."

"Clark?" Aubrey frowned. "You're attending seminary at Clark University?"

Was he in trouble? If she were standing, she'd probably have her hands on her hips. "Yes. Didn't I tell you that?"

She shook her head. "No, you only said seminary."

"Oh, I'm sorry. I guess I just assumed you knew."

"And I would know because...?"

"Well." He had to think quickly. "Mom messaging. I figured my mom told your mom, who told you." His lips twitched, hoping to ease away the irritation he heard in her voice.

She looked away and sighed before answering him. "I'm sorry I'm such a grouch, Jeremy. I guess I'm just surprised."

"You really don't like surprises, do you?" He crisscrossed his legs in front of him.

"No, not usually. I like to be first to know what's going on. But it depends on how I'm surprised."

"Maybe we can get together, eat together sometimes." Or go

on dates. Despite internal warnings, he daydreamed about spending time with her. "That should be easy, seeing we'll be on different parts of the same campus."

"That would be great, but I'll be student teaching this semester." She twirled the end of her braid. "I'll have a forty-five-minute commute."

"Oh, you know where you'll be teaching?"

"At White Mountain Elementary School. I'll be with first grade, then change to fourth. I'll be on campus on weekends. Maybe we can run together. I won't be able to do cross-country during fall semester, so running with you might be just the thing."

"We'll work something out." Maybe he shouldn't be trying so hard. Neither one of them could afford an entanglement right now.

"Aubrey White, what in the world have you done to yourself?"

The familiar voice snagged his attention.

4

"Hi, Katie." Aubrey waved.

"Jeremy, what a pleasant surprise to see you!"

Jeremy stood. Katie came up to him and put her arm around his waist.

"Hello, Red—uh, Katie." He placed his arm across her shoulders and squeezed. "It's good to see you. How have you been keeping yourself?"

"I'm fine." She bent to hug Aubrey in the lounge chair. "I came to offer my nursing services, but I see you're in good hands."

"I'm getting good care." Aubrey smiled at Jeremy over Katie's shoulder. "But I'm glad to see you. It seems news travels fast."

Katie straightened. "Well, Mom was on duty at the hospital yesterday, so she heard about your little accident."

"See, what did I tell you?" Jeremy raised his eyebrows. "Mom messaging. I have great faith in it. They get the news out fast."

Aubrey laughed at his comment, and Katie joined her. He winked at Aubrey as he resumed his seat on the grass.

"So, how's the training going?" She refocused on Katie.

"It's a lot of clinical work now." Katie settled in the grass on the other side of Aubrey. "I'll finish school in December. Then I'll have to take the state board exam." She grimaced, then smiled. "But it's worth every minute."

"You'll be a registered nurse when you finish?" Jeremy pulled up his knees.

"Yes. Mom convinced me that I should get my RN because the pay is better, and I can do more with it than an LPN. And a bachelor's degree is even better."

"You decided not to become an actress? You were quite a star in drama club."

"No." She bit her lip and her red curls bounced when she shook her head. "Acting is fun, but it wouldn't be good for me as a career. I think I'd be influenced to make bad choices in the theater. Nursing gives me the opportunity to help people. I really feel I'm doing what God intends for me to do."

Jeremy nodded. "That's good."

"Jeremy will be attending Clark Seminary." Aubrey touched his shoulder.

A tingle passed down his arm.

As though a visible spark passed between them, Katie's mouth formed an O as she looked from one to the other. "I guess you two will be seeing a lot of each other during this next school year."

"We might." Jeremy leaned back. They'd have fun together.

"We won't have much time because I'll be student teaching." Aubrey glanced at him.

Jeremy preferred to keep a positive outlook.

"How's Haleigh?" Katie asked.

How should he answer that question? "She's okay. Still taking her dog to nursing homes and hospitals, and she's on the dean's list at school."

"Has she made any plans for a career or job?"

"I don't think she knows what she'll do." How could she make plans for the future if she wouldn't let go of the past?

"I really wish ..." Katie bit her lip as her eyes met Aubrey's.
Aubrey nodded.

"I miss Haleigh." Katie rested her chin on her drawn-up knees. "Well, we can't go back to redo our lives, so we have to look forward. God is so good. In His mercy, He doesn't hold our past against us."

"I wish Haleigh would open her heart to us again too." Aubrey touched her friend's shoulder. "We've moved forward with our lives, but Haleigh seems trapped by the past. Or she's just forgotten about us."

"No." Jeremy sat up. "She hasn't forgotten. She doesn't want to deal with it. Haleigh stays busy with school, her dog, and other things so she doesn't have to think about unfinished business from the past." He shook his head. "I love my sister dearly, but sometimes she's so stubborn." He glanced from Aubrey to Katie and sighed. "At least two of the Three Sisters are moving on."

Had he said too much? He felt disloyal to speak of his sister this way. Yet, at one time, these two knew her as well as he did.

"So, Jeremy, I hear Jason's getting married."

Grateful that Katie had chosen a happier subject, he leaned back on his elbows. "Yes, next month. And then he's going to seminary closer to Carmella's hometown."

"Must be hard breaking apart the J-Brothers. They say twins have a special connection."

"True." Jeremy swatted at a fly buzzing around his face. "But we all have to grow up and move on. Carmella is a good match for him, and I know they'll be happy."

"And Mike's wedding went well?" Katie looked at Aubrey.

"Yes." Aubrey played with the sunglasses in her lap. "It was beautiful, meaningful, and fun."

Jeremy nodded. "It was. As usual, Mike set a good example for all of us."

"Mike and Madison are supposed to visit next week." Aubrey

shifted her body. "They both have good jobs and hope to buy a house soon."

"Maybe I'll get to see them." Katie stood and brushed grass off her legs. "I have to go now. I have night duty at the hospital tonight, in the emergency room." She wrinkled her nose and shook her head. "I'm not sure I'd like a permanent emergency room job. I think I'd prefer pediatrics or geriatrics."

"Whatever you do, I know you'll succeed." Aubrey held out her hand.

"Thanks, friend." Katie grasped her hand and leaned her forehead against Aubrey's. "I'll see you around. Jeremy, it was so good to see you again. Please give my love to your family."

"It was great to see you too." Jeremy stood. "And to know you're doing well. I'll give your message to my family."

"Bye." She wiggled her fingers at them, turned, and strode away.

Jeremy watched her until she turned the corner by the house. "There's only one way to describe her, full of life."

"Vivacious." Aubrey's eyes lingered on the spot where Katie disappeared. "Haleigh and I always said she was vivacious." Her smile warmed him.

He responded with one of his own.

"We both used her name in a sentence when we had *vivacious* as a vocabulary word in school. It still fits."

"I almost forgot." Jeremy checked his watch. "I have an appointment with Pastor Pete in a few minutes. Do you mind? I called him when I knew I was headed this way." He still looked forward to his meeting with Pastor Pete, but part of him wished he could stay with Aubrey.

"Oh." She shrugged. "No, that's okay. Do what you have to." She eased forward and placed her feet on the ground. "Pastor Pete went to Clark Seminary, didn't he?"

"Yes, he's one reason I decided on Clark. I'm glad he stayed on at Greenlawn Bible Church as senior pastor."

"So am I. He and Amy have a heart for the work of the church, that's for sure. They have the cutest kids." She held out her hand. "If you'll help me up, I'll go in and rest while you're gone."

"JEREMY ABBOTT." Aubrey's father entered the room. "This is an unexpected pleasure. With yesterday's excitement, my wife forgot to mention you were coming."

"It's good to see you, sir. And to be back in Greenlawn." Jeremy stood and shared a warm, firm handshake with Mr. White.

"The boys should be home any minute. Annette has thawed hamburgers, so we'll have a cookout to celebrate."

While Mr. White grilled the hamburgers, Aubrey helped her mom prepare a salad in the kitchen. Jeremy joined Willie and Jesse as they set the table on the patio and carried out the food.

After they cleaned up from supper, Aubrey invited Jeremy to take another walk.

"Do you mind if I join you?" Willie came into the living room as they prepared to leave. "I'd like to show Jeremy my work in progress."

Aubrey looked at Jeremy with eyebrows raised.

"It's fine with me. I'd like to see it." He preferred the time alone with Aubrey, but he'd like a close-up look at Willie's buildings. He'd only taken time to buy the flower for Aubrey earlier when he stopped at Willie's place.

The summer air, filled with birdsong and children's laughter, no longer held the afternoon intensity of the sun's heat. Aubrey again looped her arm through his, although she now walked without a limp. He didn't point it out, however, because he enjoyed the softness of her skin against his arm and her nearness as she walked beside him.

"I had to get a zoning variance to set up my temporary building." Willie stepped in on his other side. "I've hired a contractor to put up the buildings. Jesse has been helping me build shelves and counters when he has time."

"When do you think you'll open?"

"I plan to open the shop and greenhouse in the fall."

"I'm proud of Willie." Aubrey leaned forward to look around Jeremy at her brother. "He's worked hard to see his dream come true. He's given up vacation time and summers so he could finish college early. And now he's starting a business."

Willie grinned. "Thanks, Aubrey. I couldn't have done it without a lot of help."

The temporary building was locked up for the night. They could see the nearly completed greenhouse and the frame of the shop from the sidewalk. Willie led them underneath the orange construction tape. He allowed them to peer into the greenhouse and described the layout of the shop.

Aubrey let go of Jeremy's arm as Willie talked about his shop. Uncertain of why she let go, Jeremy flexed his arm as he dropped it to his side. Willie's business plans and the high goals he set for himself impressed Jeremy.

"Greenlawn is a small town. How do you think business will be?"

"You know how Greenlawners love their gardens. The closest florist is twenty miles away. I'm surprised someone didn't start one years ago. I know it's a risk, but it's something I want to do, and I believe God has opened this door for me."

"I'm really impressed, Willie. Thanks for showing us around."

"You're welcome. I have a few things to do here before going home. I'll see you there. Jesse mentioned a game of Monopoly."

With most of the shops closed for the night, foot and vehicle traffic were light as Jeremy and Aubrey walked back along Main Street. They stopped to look at a window display in one of the shop windows. His eyes met hers in their glass reflection.

"What are your goals, Goldie? What do you want to accomplish in the future?"

"I'll finish college, get my master's degree, and teach. Then I'll go on for my doctorate, maybe see some of the world, and become a college president. Once he gets established, Willie wants to go on short-term mission trips to teach gardening. I like Willie's idea. I'll be able to use my teaching degree almost anywhere."

Did he fit into her future?

"What about you, Jeremy?"

"I plan to finish seminary and become a pastor. Then, after that, I'll get married. Once I find the right girl." He might have found her already, but he'd still wait. He had to study hard to achieve good grades. "I'll finish my education first, so I can concentrate on one thing at a time and give it my best."

Aubrey nodded.

"I told Jason he's crazy to get married now." He shook his head. "He'll have to divide his attention between work, study, and Carmella. I think one or another will suffer from the stress."

"You're probably right." She took his arm again.

He matched his stride to hers as they turned and walked on.

"I'm glad I could stop over in Greenlawn. It's been almost like old times when the Abbotts and Whites got together."

"I'm glad you came. I didn't look forward to sitting around and amusing myself." The corners of her mouth turned up and her eyes twinkled. "Did you know you're amusing?"

She'd inherited some of her grandfather's sense of humor.

"Oh, you!" He gently pulled on her braid. He'd often teased the Three Sisters with a gentle pull on their hair. This time it was different. This time the silkiness of her hair made his fingers tingle. He let his hand glide down the braid and dropped his hand to lay on top of hers as it rested on his arm.

"I hope ... I want ..." He struggled for the right words. "What I'm trying to say is, ever since Mike's wedding, I've been thinking about us. I still have two years of seminary, and you have to finish your education ...”

“We've been friends for a long time.”

Jeremy took a deep breath and faced Aubrey. “One reason I came here today was to see you.” He grasped both her hands. She didn't pull them away. “I'm glad I came.” He licked his lips. “I think I'm falling in love with you.”

She turned her eyes downward, not at him. She stood so still, he wondered if she even breathed. Had he said it all wrong? Had he assumed too much? He held his breath.

“I'm glad you're my friend, Jeremy.” She looked into his eyes and squeezed his hands. “I like you, and I look forward to spending time with you at Clark. But I have my plans laid, and you don't know how you'll feel two years from now. I'm not ready for anything more than friendship, and I don't think you are either.” She let go of his hands.

He deflated, like a balloon leaking air. Though she hadn't rejected him entirely, she'd made her position clear. He couldn't deny that his heart's desire leaned heavily toward her right now. However, she was right, he wasn't ready. He'd have to wait for anything more.

For a while, they were quiet. Aubrey walked beside him without taking his arm. Revealing his heart to her had opened a chasm between them.

Maintaining a friendship with her would be challenging. “As friends we can hold each other accountable and keep each other on the right track.” He and Jason had always done that.

“My roommate Christina and I are accountability partners.” Aubrey nodded. “Katie, Haleigh, and I used to do that. Sometimes I wonder, if the Three Sisters had stayed together, would I have been in the accident, and would Katie have become pregnant, and Haleigh ...?”

“You feel responsible for the choices they made?”

“Sometimes. I was the oldest, the leader ...”

“I admire your sense of responsibility. You took the role of a big sister to them. But Katie's sin is not your fault, and neither is Haleigh's. They made their choices."

She looked over her shoulder when a car door slammed down the street. "I know."

"Judging from our meeting earlier, Katie's doing well. I'm sure she has her regrets, but I also noticed she hasn't been held back by her past."

"Her grandmother Whitman helped her a lot. She stayed with her grandmother during the time before the baby came. For a while, Katie thought her parents would split up, but I think her trouble woke them up. They've been a real help to her as she's finishing her education, and Katie's faith seems much stronger now." She nodded. "I think you're right. She's moving forward toward her goals."

Not like Haleigh. Would his sister remain trapped forever?

The sunset cast a pink glow over the neighborhood as they arrived back at the house.

How quickly meeting the right person could change one's point of view. He'd urged Jason to wait, to put off marriage to Carmella. Now, although he still intended to remain single until he'd completed seminary, he understood his brother's decision.

They went in to take up a Monopoly challenge with Willie and Jesse.

For a long time, Aubrey lay awake. She'd enjoyed Jeremy's visit, but she didn't regret that he'd be gone tomorrow.

It would be so easy to forget her goals and fall in love with him. But she had to live up to the White reputation.

Mike and Willie were already well on their way to making names for themselves. Everyone looked up to Mike, who excelled as a scholar, an athlete, and a Christian. Willie had pushed ahead by finishing college and starting a business before she even graduated from Clark.

The accident and Leanna's death proved how quickly opportunity, and life itself, could be snuffed out. God let her live for a reason. She had to make her life count, for her own sake and in Leanna's memory. She was a good student, and she believed God directed her in her educational path and goals for her life.

Jeremy's stated goal of finishing seminary before looking for a wife gave her time. In two years, he might find another woman who would be a better fit for him, a better pastor's wife. Her heart clenched at the thought, but she had to take that chance.

Before falling in love, getting married, and having kids, she'd make her mark in the world.

WHEN JEREMY CAME DOWNSTAIRS the next morning, he set his bag and laptop in the entryway by the front door. Aubrey hadn't come down yet. He heard the murmur of voices and entered the kitchen. Aubrey's parents sat at the table having coffee together.

"Good morning."

Both adults looked up. "Good morning, Jeremy." Mr. White nodded toward a chair. "Did you sleep well?"

"I did." Once he got to sleep. Jeremy pulled out the chair, sat down, and leaned on the table.

"Cup of coffee?" Mrs. White asked. When he nodded, she poured a mugful from the coffeemaker on the counter and set it in front of him.

"Thank you."

Mr. White opened the conversation. "We're glad you stopped to see us, and that you asked to stay overnight with us."

"I appreciate your hospitality. Thanks so much." He cupped his hands around his mug.

"You're like one of the family." Mrs. White sat next to her husband. "You're welcome any time. Did your meeting with your advisor at Clark go well?"

"Yes, I'm looking forward to attending Clark Seminary."

"What will you do, become a pastor?" Mr. White leaned forward.

"That's my intention. I feel God's leading there. Maybe church planting, or even the mission field eventually. But no matter what I do, I think Clark will help prepare me."

Mr. White nodded. "It's a good school."

Jeremy had stayed awake last night considering asking Aubrey's parents for permission to court her. But after her declaration, he knew he wasn't in her plans for the future, at least not yet.

After a brief lull in the conversation, Mrs. White said, "I know Aubrey has appreciated your company. She doesn't like to sit still, and she resents having her plans interrupted."

"I enjoyed her company." Jeremy twirled his coffee mug on the table. More than he had imagined. "She has her life goals laid out."

"Our daughter is determined to become a college president one day." Mr. White got up and poured himself another cup of coffee. "I'm not sure what drives her. I think she may still be in competition with her brothers. Mike has his dream job of coaching high school sports as he works on his graduate degree."

"Aubrey's always been competitive." Jeremy sipped his coffee.

"And you've seen Willie's business. I don't think she's jealous or angry with her younger brother, but it pushes her to try harder."

Jeremy shook his head when Mr. White held out the coffee carafe toward him.

"We're looking forward to attending Jason's wedding," Mrs. White said. "I imagine your family is excited."

"Yes, Mom likes that she'll have another daughter, and Haleigh likes the idea of evening out the number of males and females in the family."

"Madison is a great addition to our family. Aubrey gets along well with her." Mrs. White removed a bottle of orange juice from the refrigerator and filled juice glasses.

"Do you have a special girl, Jeremy?"

He gnawed his lip before answering Mr. White's question. The one he had under consideration couldn't be named. "No, not yet. I'm waiting until after seminary. That way I can concentrate on preparing for the ministry without distractions."

"That's a worthy goal." Mr. White nodded.

Aubrey's step on the stairs made his heart beat faster. He stood to greet her as she entered the kitchen.

Dressed in a jean skirt and a blue striped T-shirt, she moved gracefully, without the limp. "Good morning." Her eyes met his, then she looked from Jeremy to her parents and back. She didn't comment.

Did she suspect they'd been talking about her? They hadn't said anything bad, but her father's words gave him a better perspective on the challenge he faced with her.

Willie and Jesse joined them for breakfast, but they couldn't linger. Jeremy had to return to Wellsburg, the White men and Aubrey had to go to work, and today Mrs. White volunteered at the Greenlawn Public Library.

On the way out, Jeremy picked up his bag and laptop. Aubrey walked with him to his car. She watched him without speaking as he got into the driver's seat and closed the door. Whatever her thoughts, she didn't share them with him.

He started the car, rolled down the window, and buckled his seatbelt, wishing he still lived in Greenlawn. Then he wouldn't have to leave. The remaining weeks of summer stretched endlessly before him until he'd be with her again.

"Thank you for coming." Aubrey rested her hand on the open window. "You kept me sane yesterday."

"I'm glad I came." He placed his hand over hers, the warmth of hers seeping into his. "And I'm glad your knee is getting better. I don't think I'll be able to come here again this summer, but maybe you'll be able to come to Jason's wedding after all. We can hope." At least he did.

"I know." She looked at her watch. "I have to go to work later this morning, and you need to get on the road."

Feeling dismissed, he put on his sunglasses. "Bye, Goldie. See you soon." Her hand fell away as he shifted into reverse and backed his car out of the driveway. She lifted her hand, and he waved back.

In the side view mirror, he watched her watching him until he turned the corner.

His name came up in conversations at home, but Aubrey had to talk to someone other than her family about Jeremy. She called Christina, her college roommate and best friend. She could tell Christina things she couldn't tell anyone else.

Christina answered right away. "Hi, Roomy. I was just about to call you."

With her legs stretched out in front of her, Aubrey sat at her desk. The cut had healed, the scar beginning to fade.

"We haven't talked for a while. How's the job?" Aubrey asked.

For the summer, Christina had been hired by a couple from her church to babysit their two kids.

"The kids keep me running, but I love them. They're funny and sweet. I like that I work only Monday through Friday and have the weekends off. And the pay is good."

"I'm on the schedule at the diner for five days a week, always on Saturday so I can have Sunday off. Most weeks I work six days because Mr. Duncan calls me in to substitute for an absentee waitress."

She didn't mind staying busy and making extra money. It gave her less time to think about Jeremy and give in to the temptation to visit him in Wellsburg. If she went, she'd go to see the entire Abbot family, of course, because she wanted to maintain her *just friends* relationship with Jeremy. And Haleigh would be there.

"Daniel has texted me a few times since our Haiti trip."

Aubrey pulled her legs back and straightened in her chair. She wondered how much of her friend's conversation she'd missed as she daydreamed about Jeremy.

"We discovered we're both interested in missions." Christina had dated Daniel a few times last semester, and they both had gone to Haiti with the missions team from Clark. Christina's silence indicated her friend waited for her response.

"Is this something more than a summer romance?"

"Maybe. It's too early to say. But I really like him."

Aubrey took a deep breath. "I've met someone."

That didn't come out right. Now Christina would think she had a boyfriend. She stood and began to pace around her room.

"You have a boyfriend? Are you serious?"

"I've known him for a long time." Aubrey sat on her bed. "He used to live in Greenlawn. He came to Mike's wedding. Jeremy Abbott."

"The name sounds familiar."

"His sister and I were friends growing up. He has a twin brother, Jason. My family used to spend a lot of time with the Abbott family."

"Okay, I remember you talking about them. They sent you birthday cards. Tell me about him."

Aubrey lay back on her bed. "I don't understand it, Christina. I've known him all my life and never thought of him as more than just a friend. And I wasn't looking for anyone, you know that."

"Of course. What changed your mind?"

"I haven't changed my mind or my plans. He'll be attending Clark Seminary in the fall. He said he'd be looking for a girl to marry after he finishes seminary."

"So, if neither of you is looking for a relationship right now, what's the problem?"

"It was like a spark jumped between us when I saw him at Mike's wedding. He's not the boy next door anymore, Christina. He's six feet tall, with the Abbott chocolate brown eyes. He's sweet, thoughtful, and funny. He came to see me when he heard about my recent accident and told me he's falling in love with me. I put him off, saying we had to be just friends for now, but I can't get him out of my mind."

"Wow! I thought something must be up. I didn't think you were listening to me when I told you about Daniel and me in Haiti. How does this affect what you'll do?"

Aubrey sat up. "Oh, I haven't changed my plans. I've been researching graduate programs. My grades are good enough that I might qualify for a scholarship. There are grants available as well, especially in the area of special education.

"The website gives an application deadline by the beginning of spring term in January, and I'll have to send in my college transcript with the application. If I win one of the scholarships, I'll have to use it during the first year after obtaining my undergraduate degree."

"Will you send me the links? It's not too early to look."

"I will." She opened her laptop and sent the links to Christina. "There, you've got them."

Maybe Christina didn't understand her dilemma. If she fell in love with Jeremy, she'd fail to reach her life goals. She had to make her life count, in Leanna's memory and for herself.

"Jeremy's twin, Jason, is getting married this summer. Jeremy thinks his brother is crazy to get married before seminary. He thinks the stress of seminary along with being newlyweds is too much. He plans to finish his education first, and he knows my plans. We're friends, that's all." If she said it enough, she'd convince herself.

"I see. Will Jason be at Clark too?"

"No, he's been accepted at a seminary closer to his fiancée's hometown."

"Well, I look forward to meeting Jeremy."

Aubrey reached for the faded pink rose in the bud vase on her bedside stand. "That won't be a problem. He'll be in our neighborhood, and he wants to run at the track with us."

As expected, Aubrey didn't get time off to attend Jason Abbott's wedding. Her parents and Jesse left for the wedding on Friday afternoon, leaving Willie and her behind.

The ring tone sounded on Aubrey's phone as she let herself into the quiet house after work. Jeremy. They sent each other text messages, and occasionally they video-chatted.

"Hi, Jeremy. I'm just getting home from work."

His handsome face on the screen sent the familiar spark through her as he greeted her with a smile.

"Hi, yourself, Goldie." His smile dimmed. "I guess you didn't get the time off this weekend."

"The mother of one of the waitresses had heart surgery, so she got this weekend off. Another is a bridesmaid in her brother's wedding, so she's taking off." She kicked off her shoes and sat back against the sofa pillows with her legs up. "Willie can't take time away from his business, so it's the two of us this weekend He's trying to get his buildings finished before cold weather sets in. He's working late tonight."

"You said you probably couldn't come, but I kept hoping."

"I'd love to be there for Jason's wedding." She flexed her feet to ease the ache. "Mom, Dad, and Jesse left this afternoon. They should be there by now. At least the White family will be represented. And school will start soon. We'll see each other then."

He sighed. "I know. I still hoped to see you sooner."

Aubrey pulled her ponytail over her shoulder. "I have to work tomorrow from ten to six. I don't mind the extra hours I'm getting. I run early, while it's still cool."

"I've been running too. I've missed Jason though. He's had to stay at the camp most nights."

"How is Jason? Is he nervous?"

"No, not nervous. Excited, yes. In love, yes. And he's happier than I've ever seen him. He's had a great summer at camp. He managed to fit in all their pre-marriage meetings with Carmella's pastor. And he has everything ready to take to their new apartment after the honeymoon."

"How about you?" She detected sadness in his expression and tone of voice. "Are you okay?"

"A little sad." He shrugged. "But mostly happy for him. I think they'll find the next two years hard. I'd rather wait."

She assumed he meant he'd rather wait to get married until after seminary. That was fine with her.

"You'd be amazed at the progress Willie has made on his shop and greenhouse. Business has been good this summer, although it has slowed down a lot."

"Good for him! How about you? How's your knee?"

"All better. Only a faint scar. I could probably beat you in a race."

"Oh, you really think so?" He grinned. "We'll see about that in a couple of weeks."

In the background she heard Haleigh's voice. "Dad said to tell you it's time to go, Jeremy."

He turned his head as he spoke to his sister. "Okay. I'll be right there." He faced the screen. "The wedding rehearsal. I have to get to the church. The best man shouldn't be late."

"I wish I could be there." She'd love to witness Jason and Carmella's special time. And see Jeremy. And since Haleigh couldn't avoid attending her brother's wedding, Aubrey would've talked to her.

"I'll text you later," he said. "And I'll send you some pictures."

"Thanks, I'd like that."

They said their goodbyes, and Aubrey clicked off her phone. She relaxed against the throw pillows with her phone in her hand. Could they get married and pursue their career goals at the same time? At least one of them would have to work. Carmella planned to work while Jason attended seminary.

Would Jeremy expect the same of her? She shook her head. They hadn't even discussed getting married. Until she reached the goals she'd set for herself, anything else had to remain on the sidelines.

JEREMY CELEBRATED his twin's wedding along with his family and their friends. He took pictures with his phone to send to Aubrey. At least he wouldn't have to attempt to describe the gowns and the flowers to her. He took a couple of selfies so he could wave and smile at her.

The time passed quickly as he visited with people he knew and loved. He enjoyed meeting Carmella's gracious family. The ceremony and reception demonstrated the family's love for God and Jason and Carmella's faith. Jason had chosen well.

While his twin's bliss made him happy, loneliness enveloped him as his brother and new sister-in-law drove away after the reception. Carmella had taken first place in his brother's life, and rightly so. Jeremy didn't share confidences with his sister anymore, so he couldn't talk to her about Aubrey.

He volunteered to drive the family van home after the wedding reception. Mom and Dad fell asleep in the back seat.

"I hope Sunshine doesn't mind not taking a walk tonight." Haleigh sat in the front passenger seat. "I'll let her out in the back yard. It's late, and I'm tired."

"I think she'll understand."

"She usually does. Nadine from church has been taking care

of her while we've been gone." Jeremy nodded, his eyes on the road. "It was a beautiful wedding, wasn't it? I'm glad for Jason. It'll be fun to have Carmella for a sister-in-law. The boys don't outnumber the girls in our family now." Haleigh yawned.

"Yes, I like Carmella too."

Jeremy drove with care, watching for deer, typical on roads at night in New York, and other driving hazards. Wide awake, he decided to talk to Haleigh about Aubrey. When he started to speak, he discovered her eyes were closed. His sister had fallen asleep.

Although they arrived home in Wellsburg after midnight, Jeremy took a shower before putting on his pajamas. Everyone else went right to bed. Complete silence met his ears when he opened the bathroom door. He lay on his bed, but his body refused to relax. His brain hummed with memories of the wedding and thoughts of Aubrey.

He sent her a text message for her to read in the morning.

Using a flashlight, instead of the hall light that might disturb his sleeping family, he padded into Jason's room. His brother's packed belongings were ready to go to his new apartment after the honeymoon. Mom and Dad planned to turn Jason's room into a guest room.

A couple of books lay on top of Jason's bookcase, one on family finances and the other on having children. Jason and Carmella had used both books during premarital counseling. Jason wouldn't mind if he borrowed them.

Back in his room, he settled on his bed and turned on his bedside lamp. He leafed through the books, trying to decide which one to read first.

He lifted the photo of Aubrey from his nightstand, the one he'd taken at Mike's wedding earlier that summer. What if he asked Aubrey, and she said yes? What would it be like to come home to the woman he loved every night after seminary classes? Could they make it work?

Opening the book on finances, he began to read. His eyes got heavy. Half an hour later he awoke, set the books on the floor, Aubrey's picture on the bedside stand, and turned off his light.

The time wasn't right for more than a friend relationship with Aubrey. He knew that.

But a guy could dream, right?

6

*J*eremy watched the rain make watery patterns down his dorm room window.

Challenged by his classes, encouraged by the words and example of his professors, he knew he belonged at Clark Seminary. He'd always studied hard to earn his grades, but the immediate intensity of his course work nearly overwhelmed him.

From the text messages his twin sent him, he knew Jason experienced much the same.

Two weeks into the semester he'd managed to squeeze in only two morning runs with Aubrey because of rain. He attended two Sunday worship services with her and had three impromptu meetings with her in the campus bookstore.

He'd been right. There was no time for romance. There weren't enough hours in the day, or days in the week, for Jeremy to have the time needed with Aubrey to allow their relationship to grow and, at the same time, to give his best in preparing for ministry.

A world missions class, a meeting with his advisor, and library research filled his schedule this morning. He checked his watch.

The research for his ethics paper could be put off no longer. His outline was due by five o'clock.

Aubrey had texted that she'd be meeting with her supervising teacher at the elementary school today. She didn't say what time she'd be back on campus.

Six hours later, he called her from the seminary café while eating his evening meal.

"Jeremy, hi. How was your day?"

He pictured her shining hair and sparkling eyes. Her voice soothed away some of his stress.

"I finished my ethics outline and emailed it to my professor before five." He yawned. "How did your meeting go?"

"I really like the teacher I'll be working with, Mrs. Green. We set up the classroom, and she told me about the students. She introduced me to some of the other teachers, and we went for lunch. Then she helped me with lesson plans."

"You sound excited."

"Oh, I am. And a little nervous. I wish I didn't have to take so much time to commute."

"I'm sure you'll do well." He yawned again and blinked his tired eyes.

The background noise from Aubrey's phone increased. She must be in the Commons.

"Wow, it's noisy here! A whole bunch of students just came in to eat. I'll be at the library later. I have to do some reading and get some books."

He rubbed his eyes. "I have a meeting tonight to learn about ministry assignments, followed by a get-acquainted social hour for the teams. I'm not sure what time I'll be done. If I get out before the library closes, I'll meet you there and walk you back to your dorm."

"I'll see you then. I have a dorm meeting at ten fifteen. I'm in charge of our devotional time this week."

"Okay." He rubbed his eyes. "Will you be at the track in the morning?"

"I'll be there."

Jeremy's meeting lasted until ten. He texted an apology to Aubrey and fell into bed.

ANOTHER MORNING RUN cancelled because of the rain. Aubrey grumbled as she made her bed. Not just a shower, but a downpour!

Christina had already left the dorm room they shared to meet her boyfriend, Daniel, for breakfast.

With only a meeting with her faculty advisor today, Friday, Aubrey could go home for a weekend visit. But after driving to White Mountain Elementary School and back all week, a three-hour commute home didn't appeal to her. She wanted to attend tomorrow's home soccer match at Clark.

On gloomy days, taking extra care with her appearance usually lifted her spirits. She applied light makeup and brushed her long, blond hair back into a large barrette. From her closet she chose a light gray skirt suit with a blue blouse.

The sun burst through the clouds as she stepped outside the dorm.

After her meeting, Aubrey stopped in at one of her favorite places on campus, the bookstore. She found some red pens to use for school and a novel that a couple of her friends had recommended. She liked to have a book to read in her spare time.

A rack of fleece jackets in assorted colors, labeled "New Arrivals," caught her eye. Each had the university insignia imprinted in gold.

"The blue one. It matches your eyes."

"Oh!" Aubrey jumped and turned her head with a jerk. Her eyes connected with chocolate brown ones.

The current that passed through her left her insides shaky.

She took a deep breath and inhaled the familiar scent of his after shave. "Jeremy, you scared me."

"I'm sorry. I was trying to help you decide."

He didn't look sorry. In fact, the merry look in his eyes and the smile on his lips indicated his delight that he'd caused such a reaction from her. Like her brother Jesse. Only, she wasn't used to it from Jeremy.

"I'm just looking." She shrugged. "Grandma and Grandpa sent me some money to buy something I need or want. These jackets are new. I'm trying to decide if I really need one. And over there are corduroy jackets in University colors of burgundy and gold." She nodded toward another rack.

He stepped over to the corduroys and lifted a hanger off the rack. She moved to stand beside him.

"Don't you have a class this morning?"

"Just finished a few minutes ago. I stopped here to get a few things." He returned the hanger to the rack.

"I could have gone home for the weekend, but I'm tired of driving, and I want to go to the soccer game tomorrow." She licked her lips and took a deep breath. "Will you have time today to have lunch at the Commons with me?" Why not ask him? Friends eat together.

His face lit up. "I'd love to have lunch with you. I have to take the time to eat anyway. We haven't had much time to talk since school started, and the rain keeps interfering with our morning runs."

"My thinking too. I'll meet you at noon in front of the Commons."

"It sounds like a plan. I'll see you later."

He disappeared down the aisle he wanted, and she turned and walked to the cash register.

ON THE BENCH outside the Commons, Aubrey sat waiting. Jeremy had texted her a few minutes ago that he was on his way. She greeted friends and some professors as they passed by her on the way into the building.

Had she done the right thing to encourage Jeremy by inviting him to have lunch with her? She could have eaten with Christina and Daniel or the group of friends she often ate with in the Commons.

Jeremy strode toward her, his hair tousled. He had a habit of running his fingers through it. The rolled-up sleeves of his tan dress shirt revealed muscular forearms. He could have been dressed in a tattered t-shirt and ragged blue jeans and still be a feast for her eyes.

It was more than physical attraction. His competitive spirit turned a contest into fun because he played fairly, did his best, but didn't have to win. His determination to follow through with God's calling on his life revealed his love for God.

The intensity of her attraction surprised her. Her face heated. He'd subtly breached her defenses and found a way into her heart.

He looked thoughtful as he approached, until he saw her. A big smile spread across his face.

Excitement zinged through her when he sat beside her on the bench. She pulled her hair over her shoulder, choosing to ignore her brain's warning about commitment to her goals.

"Thanks for inviting me to have lunch with you." He left space between them, according to the campus rule of no physical contact between unmarried couples. "I have a lot of reading for the weekend, and a paper due next week. Later today I have to meet with my ministry team to plan our program for Sunday. But I needed a break." His smile always weakened her defenses.

"You look nice." His eyes flickered from her face to her clothes and back. "Your blue blouse matches your eyes. I meant to tell you that earlier."

Unable to quell the stomach flutters caused by his gaze, she smoothed her skirt with one hand. "Thank you. I'm glad you could come. I know you're busy."

Although he didn't seem to notice the many glances from the women students going in for lunch, Aubrey was quite aware of the interest he stirred. A few faculty members raised their eyebrows. They knew Aubrey as a serious student who didn't go out of her way to attract male attention. As a seminarian, Jeremy didn't spend much time on the university campus, so they didn't recognize him.

The college community resembled a small town. Everyone noticed the newcomer.

"I'm sorry." He leaned forward, folding his hands, his arms resting on his legs, and turned his face toward her. "I want to have more time with you, but the profs are piling on the work. I can't seem to get ahead, and our schedules don't match."

"I know. That's all right. You're not obligated to spend time with me. But why not have lunch together?"

"Why don't we go in, then we can talk." He looked over his shoulder as a noisy group of students approached, then pushed the lock of hair on his forehead to the side and stood.

Jeremy held the door open for her, and she led the way into the food line. Aubrey pointed out some empty seats in a quieter corner of the full, noisy dining room.

As they ate and talked, she lost track of time. Silence fell, and she looked around. Except for Jeremy and her, no one sat at any of the tables.

"How long have we been here like this?" She whispered as her eyes met Jeremy's.

"I have no idea."

Without another word, they got up and placed their lunch trays on the conveyor belt for the dishwasher.

"Sorry," they said together to the student worker.

"About time." He scowled at them.

As they walked out into the late summer sunshine, Aubrey stifled an embarrassed giggle.

"Why is it, when I'm with you, two hours seems like ten minutes?" Jeremy's voice echoed her unexpressed thoughts. "Maybe it's better we don't spend more time together. I'm not sure I'd get any studying done,"

"Maybe it's because ..." Aubrey stopped. Instead of saying *we love each other*, she said, "Maybe it's because we like to talk."

He bent close to her ear. "What were you going to say, Goldie?" His breath against her ear made her shiver.

Saying the words might change everything.

Thoughts of him invaded her mind at unexpected moments, his handsome face, his strong hands, his chocolate eyes. She couldn't deny a growing love for him, deeper than friendship. His sense of humor made her laugh, and his faith encouraged hers.

Until the spark between them at Mike's wedding ignited dreams of a future with Jeremy, her goal had been her career as a teacher and beyond. Still was. A White always followed through with goals.

Besides, he'd already committed himself to wait two years.

Those words could wait for now.

She pulled her hair over her shoulder. "I'll be at the track in the morning. Will you be able to meet me there?" Would he let her change the subject?

"It's a date." He straightened. "How about we go to the soccer game tomorrow afternoon? I hear Clark University has a good soccer team."

Though she'd planned to go with Christina and Daniel, it would be fun to go with Jeremy too. They shared a love for the sport.

"Will that give you enough time to study?"

"I'll just have to burn an extra candle." He shrugged. "I need a break. I can't think of a better way to do it than with you."

His warm gaze confirmed his words. Heat spread through her. He made time for what was important to him, and she was important to him.

"Thank you, Jeremy. It will be fun going with you."

Puffy white clouds floated in the azure sky. The campus shimmered in the glow of the sunshine and changing leaves, mirrored by the glow in her heart as she sauntered along the sidewalk with him.

They sat in the gazebo in front of the fine arts building and talked.

Jeremy checked his phone. "Oh, no, I have to go to my meeting." He stood. "I've really enjoyed our time together."

"So have I. I'm meeting Christina and Daniel for supper later, and then we're going to the student center for a foosball tournament. Do you want to come?" With his seminary ID, he'd be able to get in with her.

"It sounds great, Goldie, but I'll have to say no. I have to get some reading done tonight. I'm sorry."

"No, that's all right. I thought I'd ask." Her disappointment at his refusal was greater than she expected.

The invitation had been impulsive. Why would a seminary student want to spend an evening with a bunch of undergraduates?

Aubrey stepped out of the gazebo and waited for Jeremy to join her. "Christina and I have volunteered at a nursing home, Bible Clubs, and Sunday School to fulfill our ministry requirement each semester. Our track coach has connections with someone from Special Olympics, so the team sometimes works with kids with disabilities as they train. What will you do as a ministry team?"

"Churches within a hundred-mile radius of Clark invite seminary students to be a part of their ministerial and Christian education staff for a semester, often in teams. Tonight, we get our assignments."

"You sound excited about it."

"I am." He nodded. "Except ..." He stopped, and she did too. He turned to face her, his hands stuffed in his pockets. "Except there may be times when I'll have to go on Friday night and won't be back until Sunday night. It'll depend on what the church has on its calendar."

"Oh, I thought ..." She'd looked forward to weekends with Jeremy. However, that wasn't her purpose for being at Clark. She buried her disappointment and shrugged. "We're both here to prepare for the future. I'm sure we'll find other times to be together."

A challenge would lighten the moment. "I'll meet you at the track at six-thirty sharp tomorrow morning, with running shoes on."

"You're on, Goldie." He gave her a thumbs-up. "We'll have fun together tomorrow."

She watched as he hurried away from her toward the seminary campus. Just by being Jeremy, he made it hard for her to resist him.

LIFE HAD BECOME MORE complicated with Aubrey in the picture. It would have been easier to stick to his original plan if that spark hadn't ignited his growing attachment to her and if he hadn't chosen to attend Clark Seminary.

Jeremy ran to get to his meeting on time, swerving off the sidewalk into the grass to avoid colliding with other students.

He'd committed the next two years to prepare for God's service, and she planned to get her master's degree. With all he had to do right now, how could he give a woman like Aubrey the time and attention she deserved? Could either of them afford to be distracted by falling in love?

No, he had to follow his original plan.

Slowing to a jog as he approached the seminary chapel building, he pulled out his phone. Good, five minutes to spare before his meeting.

He stepped to the side of the doorway to allow other students to enter as he texted Jason, requesting a video chat later that night or in the morning. Time and distance prevented him from getting together with his twin until Haleigh's birthday in November, but he needed his brother's advice sooner than that.

He entered the building. Right now, he had a meeting to attend. Tomorrow he'd see Aubrey. The rest ... in God's hands.

7

The day awakened around Aubrey as she turned her car onto the highway. She sang along with her favorite Christian group on the radio.

Aubrey preferred early mornings to late nights. Even so, it took two weeks for her to perfect her morning routine so she'd arrive at White Mountain Elementary School half an hour before students. Thanks to a shortcut the first-grade teacher, Mrs. Green, had told her about, she pulled into the parking lot after thirty-five rather than forty-five minutes.

A sunny day meant the students could play outside during recess and expend some of their boundless energy. Especially Kenny Jones, who reminded her of her brother Jesse.

Carrying her purse, her briefcase, and a large shopping bag, she entered the classroom. "Good morning."

Mrs. Green looked up from her desk. "Good morning, Miss White. I see you came prepared for your last day in first grade."

"The time has passed so quickly I can hardly believe it's my last day with you."

Aubrey set the bag and briefcase beside her desk then hung her coat in the closet and locked her purse in the bottom drawer of her desk.

"The students are going to miss you. They've enjoyed learning from you."

"I've learned so much from you and from them."

"They require a lot of patience from us because we're laying the foundation for the rest of their learning as they develop basic skills in things like reading, writing, and math. They're beginning to learn the why and how of the world around them. Some of them are eager to learn, and others—not so much."

Like Kenny. From the initial day of first grade, he'd declared he didn't like school. He had trouble concentrating in class, and his numerous antics brought laughter to the classroom. Sometimes Aubrey had to cover her mouth and turn away to hide her smile when Mrs. Green reprimanded him.

"Every day brings a new challenge." Mrs. Green checked her watch. "Now, we'd better make sure we're ready. The students will be arriving soon."

Aubrey greeted each student at the door with a high-five or hug. Of course, Kenny jumped up as he gave her a high-five. Then he surprised her with a hug. He skipped into the classroom, hung up his coat, took papers and books from his backpack, and sat at his desk. Was he ill?

"Good morning, Miss White." A petite girl with brown hair and dark brown eyes hugged her.

"Good morning, Serena."

Serena reminded Aubrey of Jeremy's sister, Haleigh. She struggled with making friends and seldom spoke without being called on in the classroom, even when she knew the answer to a question. However, she enjoyed reading, always completed her homework, and loved to learn.

When Aubrey returned to her desk after noon recess, a milky, white stone lay on her desk. Kenny smiled shyly when she caught his eye.

She walked over and crouched beside his desk. "Kenny, is this stone from you?"

"Do you like it?" His face held a worried expression.

"Of course I do! It's a beautiful gift. Thank you."

"It's a white stone." His face brightened with a broad grin.

"You mean like my name."

He nodded. "I found it at Grandma's, and she said I could have it."

"I'll treasure it. Thank you."

The afternoon passed quickly. For her last activity with the first grade, Aubrey helped them make peanut butter pinecone feeders for the wild birds, something she had enjoyed as a child. In groups of four, she taught them how to spread peanut butter all over the cones, then roll them in birdseed.

"Miss White," said Kenny as he carefully spread the peanut butter, "if I be good, will you stay?"

"What do you mean, Kenny?"

"I don't want you to leave."

"Is that why you've been so quiet today?" Aubrey crouched beside him. "Kenny, I'm not leaving because you're bad. I'm going to help in fourth grade starting next week."

"But, why?"

"Well, you won't stay in first grade forever. You'll move on and learn more. I have a lot more to learn about teaching."

Next week she'd broaden her learning experience by transferring to a fourth-grade class with Mrs. Breck. She looked forward to it.

But she didn't look forward to another weekend without Jeremy. He had to leave with his ministry team tonight and wouldn't return until Sunday night. Finding a balance in her relationship with him continued to challenge her.

At least she'd signed up to go with the track team tomorrow to work with special needs athletes, something she always enjoyed.

AFTER WORKING with the special needs athletes for several hours, Aubrey and Christina were now on their way back to the Clark campus. They sat together on the bus with the women's track team as they ate the bag lunches provided by the university cafeteria.

"I miss my early morning workouts on the track." Aubrey reached into her bag and pulled out two cookies wrapped in plastic. Judging from the scent of peanut butter that filled her nostrils, they must be peanut butter cookies. Did she want to eat them?

Christina wiped her fingers on her napkin. "Me too. At least we can still run after school."

"If the weather cooperates, and I don't have to stay after school."

From the corner of her eye, she could see her roommate staring at her. She turned her head and met Christina's gaze.

"What?"

"You're Miss Sunshine today. What's up with you? "

"What do you mean?" Aubrey knew what her friend meant. She didn't like to whine, but that's exactly how she sounded to herself.

"Well?" Christina wouldn't let her off easily. They'd been roommates and friends for a long time.

She tossed the cookies back in the bag. "I hardly ever see Jeremy. We can't run together mornings. If I have to stay late after school, or he has a meeting or lecture to attend, we have to be satisfied with a phone call or text message. I have school all day when he might have some free time.

"We can't do anything together on weekends because his ministry team works at a church over an hour away. Sometimes he's gone from Friday until Sunday night."

"Oh, so that's what's bothering you." Christina took a bite of a cookie. "These are good, Aubrey."

"That's all you can say?" Christina's lack of sympathy irritated her. "You see Daniel every day. You don't understand."

"Maybe I don't understand what you're going through with Jeremy." Christian shrugged. "Why does it matter anyway? You told me neither of you wanted a relationship right now. But the track team and the kids we worked with didn't deserve your grouchiness. Why did you bother to come today?"

That hurt! She bit back an angry reply. Christina was right. She'd been distracted and impatient and had taken out her bad attitude on those around her.

"I'm sorry, Christina. You're right. It's not your fault. I owe a lot of people apologies. This is something I have to pray about."

If she and Jeremy were just friends, why did it matter?

THE MAN LEANED FORWARD. "My daughter is not a bully! You lie!" He pointed at her, his face red.

Aubrey stiffened, thankful for the table between them. She prepared to defend her actions. Mrs. Breck, the fourth-grade teacher with whom she now worked, laid her hand on Aubrey's arm.

"Mr. Stevens, please lower your voice and remember you're in a school," Principal Marks said. "I know you're angry, but please listen to Mrs. Breck before you judge."

As he tried to defuse the tense atmosphere, Aubrey appreciated his intervention. He'd already listened to her explanation.

The father sat back with his arms folded and pressed his lips together, as though daring anyone to contradict him.

Aubrey licked her lips and took a deep breath, praying for her supervising teacher. She'd given Mandy detention, in accord with the school disciplinary handbook. Gratitude filled her that Mrs. Breck stood up for her.

"I'm not sure what Mandy told you, Mr. Stevens." Mrs. Breck leaned toward Mandy's father across the table and began with a positive. "You obviously care about her, or you wouldn't be here."

Mandy's father shifted slightly, relaxing a bit.

"The students were busy with seat work, and the room was quiet." The teacher continued. "Mandy sits in the middle of the room, and Greg's seat is in the next row. She spoke quietly, but Miss White heard her, a swear word and a terrible name."

Would this be the end of her teaching career? Aubrey cringed as Mr. Stevens's eyes narrowed.

"I heard Miss White speak to Mandy, and I saw Greg's face. I think a few other students heard Mandy because they looked shocked. Mandy denied having said anything at all, but she was caught in the act. We simply kept her in at recess, and Miss White tried to talk to her."

He stiffened and glared at Aubrey. "I don't believe she said what you claim she said."

Aubrey sucked in a breath as Mrs. Breck continued. "Mr. Stevens, I found it hard to believe that Mandy would use such language. But you must understand, Greg Adams is a special student. He has hydrocephalus."

"What's that?" Mr. Stevens frowned.

"Greg's head is enlarged because of excess fluid in his brain. Mandy's words referred to his physical appearance."

Principal Marks nodded. "Mrs. Breck supports Miss White's allegations. She suspected Mandy of saying disparaging things to Greg, but she couldn't catch her doing it. You already know your daughter's behavior this semester has created some problems in the classroom. Bullying is against our school's policy, Mr. Stevens. Perhaps you should set up an appointment to talk with Mrs. Breck about Mandy."

"We've been planning to do that." The man's defensive attitude melted away. "Things have been a bit hectic at home lately." He leaned forward and looked at his hands folded on the table. The dark circles under his eyes indicated stress or lack of sleep.

"I'm sorry, Miss White, that I jumped at you that way. I should have listened to both sides before assuming you were to blame. Mandy said she got detention and that you picked on her." His shoulders slumped and his mouth turned down.

Aubrey felt sorry for him. She'd heard that his wife had been diagnosed with breast cancer. Perhaps that and a relaxing of discipline in the home had caused Mandy's problem. She believed the authenticity of his apology.

Aubrey took a deep breath. "May I say something?"

"Of course." Principal Marks nodded to her.

"Mr. Stevens, I'm sorry that Mandy felt picked on. I only wanted to help her and Greg."

"I know." He sighed.

The teacher and the principal stood. Aubrey, her legs shaking, got up from her chair.

"I'll see you ladies out. Mr. Stevens, I'll be right back." Mr. Marks escorted Aubrey and Mrs. Breck to the outer office, closing the door behind him.

Aubrey's hands shook, her legs wobbled, and her stomach fluttered. Keeping Mandy in at recess to talk to her was a proper disciplinary action, but Mr. Stevens's anger had frightened her. She didn't know if it had been worse being questioned by the principal or being yelled at by the father.

"There are many facets to education, and one of them is irate parents." Mr. Marks turned to Aubrey. "I've known the Stevens family for a long time. He can be hot-headed at times. It's best to try to stay calm."

"I prayed." Maybe she shouldn't have said that. "Thank you for your support and Mrs. Breck's. I only followed handbook procedure."

"Yes, you did." He looked at the clock. "Your students should be returning from recess. You may go back to your class now."

"Oops!" Aubrey nearly bumped into Mrs. Breck, who paused in the doorway to say one more thing to the principal.

"Thank you for your help, Mr. Marks. I hope Mandy's parents will make an appointment to talk with me."

"I'll see that they do." he said.

The roomful of energetic fourth graders to which she returned bubbled over with excitement as they prepared for their upcoming school play. She remained after school to help two students who'd fallen behind in their English grammar assignments.

Would the day ever end?

"Finally!" Aubrey pulled into her dorm parking space and turned off the car. She leaned her head back against the seat, closed her eyes, and took three deep, cleansing breaths. If it weren't so late, she'd go for a run. She needed it. She'd just experienced the worst day of her life. At least it felt that way. Maybe the second worst.

The worst had been the day she woke up in the hospital after her accident, with physical pain, terrifying dreams, and learning of Leanna's death.

The high point of her day today had been Greg himself.

'Have a nice weekend, Miss White,' he'd said with his sweet, bright smile, as he left that afternoon. 'I'll see you Monday.'

She smiled. Maybe it hadn't been her second worst day after all. She pulled the key out of the ignition, picked up her purse, and opened the car door. Beside her car, she breathed in the cool evening air. The moon appeared, a tiny sliver of light in the blue-black sky. The first stars twinkled in the dark expanse overhead. A perfect night for a walk on campus with Jeremy. Except he wasn't there.

Several sets of papers to correct this weekend waited in her briefcase. Next weekend she'd go home for a visit, after a meeting on Friday with her advisor. She wouldn't have to return to campus until Monday because of the public school holiday.

Aubrey wanted to talk to her advisor about getting her master's degree in special education. Her work with the young athletes with physical challenges, and Greg's smile, cheerful attitude, and the challenges he faced cemented her desire to teach special needs kids.

Because of his ministry team, Jeremy wouldn't have time for her this weekend.

It wasn't his fault. She shook her head. But as the semester progressed, she saw less and less of him.

"It just isn't our time, I guess," she whispered to herself.

8

"Hi, Roomy, you're late tonight." Christina greeted her as she entered their shared room. "Problems at school?" The dark-haired young woman leaned over the dresser, looking into the mirror as she applied makeup.

"Just one of those days." Aubrey wanted to pour out her student teacher problems to Christina, but lately she'd complained a lot. She set her briefcase on her desk and flopped across her bed. "You have a date with Daniel tonight?"

Christina nodded. "Yes. How about you?"

"No." Aubrey sighed and closed her eyes. "Jeremy's team had to leave today. Maranatha, the church where they work, is having special activities for teens this weekend, so he won't be back until Sunday night."

"I'm sure Daniel could find a friend, and we could double-date." Christina looked at her in the mirror.

Aubrey considered Christina's offer. In the past they'd occasionally double-dated. A couple of guys had asked her out this semester, but she'd made her excuses.

The thought of dating someone other than Jeremy made her feel disloyal, even though she and Jeremy had no official understanding. Even though she tried to convince herself they were just friends.

After experiencing the ups and downs of three years of college together, she knew a refusal wouldn't hurt Christina's feelings.

"No thanks, Christina." Keeping her voice calm, she shook her head. "Not tonight. I'll be fine. I'm going to change and scoot over to the Commons before it closes."

Christina looked over her shoulder. "You know, the campus rumor mill has you connected to this good-looking seminary student."

"So?" Aubrey shrugged. That didn't bother her as much as it should have. "I've had a tough day, and I'm tired."

"Okay. Maybe another time."

"Thanks anyway." Aubrey stood. "Have a good time with Daniel."

She ate with several friends in the dining hall. Afterward, she joined them at the student center, just hanging out, talking and laughing, playing Dutch Blitz. When she returned to her room relaxed and refreshed, Christina hadn't returned, so she called Jeremy.

Just when she expected to connect with his voice mail, he finally answered. A blast of background noise made her hold the phone away from her ear.

"Hi, Aubrey." He spoke loudly. "We're not finished here. That's why I didn't call."

"Wow!" She raised her voice. "What's going on?"

"They're eating pizza," he shouted back. "We had a wild volleyball tournament earlier."

"Must be a whole multitude of teens there. I can hardly hear you. They're actually eating and still making that much noise?"

"Oh, Jeremy." A female voice sang out.

A jab of jealousy pierced her insides at the voice in the background. "Who's that?" It was probably one of the team members, Renée or Sarah.

"I'll be there in a minute," he said more quietly, then shouted into the phone, "Aubrey, I'll call you later, okay? There's too much noise, and I have to go."

Aubrey paused. "Oh, okay. That might be better." She sighed.

"Is something wrong?" he asked.

If she complained about her bad day, she'd be whining. "No. I know you're busy. Call me back when you can. I'll be here. 'Bye." She clicked off the phone before giving him time to say anything more. She could manage this on her own.

The background noise, the woman's voice, and his obvious preoccupation soured her mood. He'd have to call her back when he had time.

Aubrey set her alarm clock so she'd be able to get up and run before breakfast. She'd correct test papers and read compositions about pets in the morning. In the afternoon she'd go to the last soccer game of the season, probably with Christina and Daniel. She tried to read for a while before going to sleep.

But when Christina came in just before curfew, she awoke with the book beside her on the bed. Jeremy hadn't called back after all, and she was too sleepy to check for a text message.

JEREMY PUNCHED HIS *OFF* KEY. Aubrey had ended the call abruptly before he could even ask about her day. He really wanted to talk with her, but he had to get back to work. She understood that, right? The kids should be gone in another hour. Then he'd call her.

If only Sarah hadn't called out to him in such a flirty voice while he talked to Aubrey. Maybe Sarah hadn't meant anything by it, thought it was cute or funny. One more thing to clear up with Aubrey when he called her later.

Pocketing his phone, he searched the sea of bodies for Sarah. Where had she gone, and what did she want?

"Jeremy!"

Was he hearing things? It was hard to tell in the noisy gymnasium.

"Jeremy!"

He whirled around and spotted Matt, the Maranatha youth pastor, motioning to him over the heads of a circle of kids. With multiple apologies, he pushed his way through the crowd. Jeremy gasped.

Inside the circle of teens, a boy lay on the floor, his face pale, his eyes closed. Jeremy recognized him, but he wasn't a regular at Maranatha. Matt and another adult knelt beside him.

"He passed out." Matt stood. "But he's coming around now. His youth leader has called his parents. I'm taking him to the emergency room and want you to go with me."

"All right. Just let me tell Kyle where I'm going, so he won't look for me." He'd ridden to the event with his ministry team in Kyle's car.

"Where did you go, Jeremy?" Sarah stopped him as he headed toward Kyle. "Lindsey's ankle is swelling. I think she sprained it playing volleyball."

Lindsey, a teen girl from Maranatha, limped up, supported by two other girls. One glance at Lindsey's pain-filled face and her red, swollen ankle supported Sarah's suspicions.

"Take her over to Matt. I'm going with him to take a boy to the emergency room, but I have to tell Kyle."

"I'll tell Kyle. You take Lindsey."

"Thanks, Sarah."

Half an hour later, Lindsey's parents met them at the emergency room. The father of the boy, Caleb, arrived soon after that. X-rays confirmed Lindsey's sprain, and a doctor had determined that Caleb had passed out from dehydration. Jeremy and Matt spoke to the parents and prayed with the teens, then returned to Maranatha.

The grandfather clock struck one o'clock as he entered the deacon's house, where he and Kyle stayed on weekends.

Too late to call Aubrey now. He ran his fingers through his

hair. She liked to go to bed early so she could get up early in the morning to run before breakfast, and Jeremy didn't want to disturb Aubrey's roommate. Hoping they could talk soon, he sent her a text message.

He lay in bed, seeing her sparkling blue eyes and shining hair. Her voice and laughter echoed in his mind. For the amount of time they had together, he might as well be on his way to the moon.

At the beginning of the semester, he'd been convinced he would marry Aubrey one day. Tonight, she seemed so far away. Was God sending them in different directions?

THE NEXT MORNING, Aubrey read his message. She responded, 'I see you were busy. We can talk later.'

She left her phone charging while she ran, then forgot to take it when she went to breakfast at the Commons, where she ate with Christiana and Daniel and several other friends.

"Hey, Aubrey, where's that cute seminarian I saw you with at the game a few weeks ago?" Olivia asked.

Aubrey shrugged, using her mouth full of food as an excuse not to answer.

"Tall, dark, and handsome. Jeremy Abbott, right?" Eleanor sighed and fluttered her lashes. "Do you have a date tonight?"

Normally she would have laughed because she knew they only teased in fun. But the memory of her phone call with him last night, and the woman's flirty voice calling him, stuck with her. Her face heated, and she bit her lip to keep back an angry response.

"No, he's away with his ministry team this weekend."

From the corner of her eye, she saw Christina shake her head at the girls.

Daniel cracked a joke, and she joined in the laughter that

followed. That set off a round of jokes and laughter which lightened her mood.

When she returned to her room, she discovered she'd missed Jeremy's call. He didn't leave a message.

"Oh, great!" She didn't feel like talking to him right now anyway. Besides, he was probably busy, and she had work to do.

Maybe it was time to let her relationship with Jeremy cool. She'd already allowed her heart to become too entangled.

The walls of her room closed in on her. Hopefully, at the University library she could contain her restlessness while isolated at a study carrel without distractions. She checked her briefcase to be sure she had everything she needed.

Aubrey enjoyed teaching and loved her fourth-grade students. She appreciated the insights of her supervising teacher and mentor, Mrs. Breck, and felt comfortable working with and learning from her.

Most of the students did well or as expected on the tests, but she shook her head at Mandy's. In the past month, Mandy's grades had plummeted. The girl needed help. She hoped Mr. Stevens had made that appointment with Mrs. Breck.

As she read the compositions, she smiled. By the way they expressed themselves, the words they used, the way they formed their sentences, Aubrey heard each child's voice through their writing. There were the usual spelling and grammar errors, but they had to learn through practice.

The bright sunshine and crisp autumn air lifted Aubrey's spirits when she exited the library. She climbed the steps to the next level of the campus, where she could look out over the valley below. Most of the colorful leaves had dropped from the trees, but there were still some coppers, golds, and bronzes. She leaned against the stone wall in front of her.

The day reminded her of Haleigh Abbott, who shared a love for nature with her grandmother. Dear Gram. Haleigh 's connection with her grandmother had been close, and she had probably suffered more than anyone else when Gram passed away. That happened soon after Aubrey's accident.

She and Katie had visited Haleigh together one last time when they heard about Haleigh's puppy. It was a day much like today, with bright sunshine and autumn leaves. The smile that lit Haleigh's face when she saw them made Aubrey ashamed she hadn't taken more time for her.

As the three girls sat together on the living room floor, the little, black puppy ran from one to the other, sniffing, licking, wagging her tail and the back half of her body. She and Katie both laughed at the puppy's name: Sunshine. The name fit though, because Sunshine, with her sweet personality and her funny antics, made her feel happy.

Aubrey wanted to remain friends with Haleigh, but other friends, especially Leanna, and sports took up much of her time in high school. Leanna mostly ignored Haleigh. Haleigh participated in sports only in gym class or a youth group activity. Their diverging interests and Haleigh's refusal to accept the changes broke their friendship.

A cool breeze brushed Aubrey's face, bringing her back to the present.

Her broken relationship with Haleigh mattered more now because, against her better judgment and contrary to her goals, she'd fallen in love with Haleigh's brother.

Wow! Here she was, acting like Haleigh, upset because Jeremy had other things to do.

"Are you here or somewhere else, Aubrey?" A male voice startled her.

"Oh!" Aubrey jumped. "Oh, hi, Mac." She brushed a few hairs away from her face. "Just reminiscing."

The tall, thin, young man standing beside her wore a Kelly-green shirt, which made him quite visible and complemented his red hair. Mac loved bright colors. She appreciated his spiritual insights and sense of humor and considered him one of her best friends on campus, though they'd never be more than friends.

Mac, also a senior education major, did his student teaching at a different school. Aubrey had talked to him only a few times in the Commons this semester.

"I don't ever remember seeing you just standing around." He leaned against the wall. "You're always doing something."

"I have my moments." She gestured at the scenery with her hand. "Isn't this a beautiful day?"

"We won't have many more like today this year. Hard to believe it's already November. How's your student teaching going?"

Aubrey told him about little Kenny and Serena in first grade, and Mandy and Greg in fourth grade, as they walked toward the Commons to get lunch. When her phone vibrated, Aubrey looked at it. Jeremy.

"Excuse me." She held up her phone. Mac nodded and continued on his way, as she turned aside to stand in the grass and answer her phone.

"Hi, Jeremy." She tried to maintain her lighter mood and keep the tone of her voice cheerful. The thought of being pushed aside by one of his team members last night when she called still irked her.

"Hi, yourself. About last night: I hope you didn't think I wanted to cut you off."

She shook her head and then remembered he couldn't see her. "No, I knew you were busy." She knew, but she'd been irritated and jealous and probably owed him an explanation of why she hadn't called him back. "I didn't get your text until this morning. You had a rather eventful evening, I guess."

"Yes, and it was quite late when I finally got in."

"How are the kids?"

"Well, the girl has to stay off her ankle for a couple of days, and the guy was better after they hydrated him in the emergency room." He paused. "What are you doing now?"

Here was her opportunity to tell him about her bad day yesterday. Contrariness, however, took over. "Oh, I'm just standing here talking on the phone to you. I'll be heading for the Commons for lunch. How about you?"

"The ministry team will be meeting at the pastor's house for lunch and to get ready for the youth rally tonight. They've invited a motivational speaker, and we expect about 500 teens from the area. We're meeting in the local high school auditorium."

"You sound really excited." Aubrey stepped back to the sidewalk and headed for the Commons. His excitement made her want to be part of the action.

"Wow, Aubrey, it's great! I wish you could be here with me. You'd love it!"

His words echoed her own desire, lessened her irritation. She didn't offer a response, however.

"Let's plan to run together next week."

"Afraid not." Aubrey shook her head. "I have to put in extra time after school on Monday, Tuesday, and Wednesday to get ready for a school play on Thursday evening. It will be too late to run by the time I get home. On Monday night, Christina and I have a commitment at Terrace Baptist Church, and I promised Christina I'd attend a mission's department function with her on Tuesday."

"Maybe we can eat together on Friday at the seminary café."

"I'm going home next weekend. My school has a four-day weekend, and this will be my first time at home since I started student teaching, except for one quick overnight. I'll leave Friday morning and won't be back until Monday night. But the following weekend I'll probably be free."

His silence worried her.

"Are you still there?"

"I'm here, Aubrey. The following weekend I have to go to Wellsburg for Haleigh's twenty-first birthday. I'll be leaving after class on Friday, and I plan to go right from Wellsburg to Maranatha on Sunday morning."

"Oh, I'd forgotten about Haleigh's birthday."

"I know what!" His voice oozed excitement. "You can go with me. My family will be glad to see you and—"

"I don't think so, Jer."

"Why not?"

"Because it's your sister's birthday. I don't want to ruin her special day by crashing her party."

"You won't be crashing her party. You'll be my guest. Haleigh will be glad to see you. I know she will."

Aubrey paused outside the Commons. "Haleigh has refused to talk to me, write me, or call me since your family left Greenlawn. I can't force myself on her. Maybe one day we'll be able to talk things out, but not now." Frustration spilled over into her words with Jeremy. He didn't understand he couldn't force her reconciliation with Haleigh.

And she certainly didn't want tension between her and Haleigh to ruin an Abbott family celebration.

"Please, Goldie. It will give us the chance to be together."

"I know." She agreed with him on that point. Time together had taken a low position on their priorities' list. She almost gave in to his pleading. "But not this time." Changing the subject might distract and calm him. "I'm sorry you'll miss the soccer game this afternoon. This is the last one for the season."

"All right, Aubrey. But if you change your mind, the offer is still open." His tone had become cool.

She'd hurt his feelings.

"I'm sorry I can't go to the game with you." Voices echoed in the background from his phone. "I have to go now. May I call you tonight?"

"Yes. I'll be here."

How did a phone call from Jeremy turn into an argument? She stared at her phone after the call ended. The tension between them nearly crackled.

If love made you so out of sorts and grumpy, she didn't want it. Love should make you happy, right?

Discouraged, Aubrey entered the dining hall and joined the

lunch line. She needed the break next weekend. No homework, no papers to correct.

Later today she'd slip into the University chapel alone and pray, get her life, goals, and relationship with Jeremy into proper perspective.

HOW COULD SHE DO THAT? Jeremy had found the perfect solution to their lack of time together, and Aubrey had refused him. And he'd lost the opportunity to heal the breach between the girl he loved and the sister he loved.

"I wish I understood her better," he muttered.

Since the beginning of the semester, he'd sensed the dismantling of her wall of resistance to him. However, he had less and less time for her. His weekends at Maranatha meant he spent more time during the week on his course work. She had dorm and campus activities, and she sometimes stayed late for concerts and plays at the elementary school.

Going with him to visit his family would be a perfect solution. They'd have the weekend together, and she could go with him to Maranatha on Sunday.

At times like this he especially missed Jason. Though they texted, connected on social media, and called each other occasionally, he looked forward to finding a few free minutes to speak to his twin. During his time in Wellsburg two weekends from now, a heart-to-heart was in order.

"Let it go, Abbott." He had to focus on getting ready for the youth rally tonight.

That evening, the motivational speaker had the kids mesmerized with his message of encouragement and faith. Jeremy needed the message too.

The excitement of being part of this youth outreach couldn't totally overcome the heaviness he carried in his heart because of Aubrey. If only he could find a simple solution.

9

On Monday, Aubrey came up with a partial solution to their time problem. She invited Jeremy to the elementary school play on Thursday evening.

"I'd like for you to come." Again, she spoke to him over the phone. She'd been late getting back, and he had to study for a test. "That way you can meet my students and some of the people I work with."

"I'll plan on it. I'll look forward to seeing you and the play."

On Thursday morning she texted him.

Looking forward 2 today.

He responded.

C u 2 night.

She wore a blue dress because he always said the color matched her eyes, and she took special care with her hair, pulling it back at the sides and leaving it long down her back, the way he liked it. She could hardly wait to introduce him to Mrs. Breck and the students, especially Greg, and for him to see her in action in her chosen profession as a teacher.

Thursday afternoon, she stayed at school taking care of last-minute details for the performance.

As the time for the opening curtain drew near, she watched for him. He never showed. No call or text to say he'd be late. Had he forgotten? She pictured him hurt in an accident but managed to suppress her fear and tears and gave her full attention to helping the students.

The children performed well. The parents thanked her, and Mrs. Breck commended her hard work.

She hid her disappointment until she sat behind the steering wheel of her car, ready to return to campus. In the darkness, she allowed the tears. Jeremy must have forgotten, or he found something more important to do. Or maybe he stood her up because she refused go to Wellsburg with him. She wiped away her tears. She wouldn't cry. If she'd stuck to her original plan, she wouldn't have this mess now.

And God didn't seem to be sending any answers her way.

SARAH ASKED Jeremy to meet with her Thursday evening to plan a young adults' Sunday school class they were assigned to team teach on Sunday. Jeremy checked his phone calendar. Finding nothing else on his schedule, he agreed.

As much as possible, he avoided meeting one-on-one with Sarah. They met in the student lounge next to the seminary café, a place frequented by other seminarians. He didn't want Sarah, or anyone else, to think they were a couple.

Afterwards, he called Aubrey, but she didn't answer. She didn't respond to his voice mail message or his text message.

He'd met her only once during the week, in the campus bookstore, and had spoken to her on the phone once. If only he could figure a way to relieve the tension between them.

Hoping to see her before she left for home, he texted her first thing on Friday morning. Several times during the day, he texted her again and tried to call her. Every call went to voice mail. She never responded.

Even the three-hour drive to Greenlawn wouldn't prevent her from texting or calling at a rest stop or from home.

Friday night, and he couldn't concentrate on the paper he had to write. He pushed back from his computer and stood up.

Everything had been so clear during the summer. Now he wondered. Why did she refuse to go to Wellsburg with him? Was it really because she didn't want to upset Haleigh, or did she not want to be with him?

No, Aubrey said what she meant.

He called her again, this time not leaving a message.

"Forget it!" His worry turned into anger. "If she doesn't have time for me, I have better things to do." He ran his fingers through his hair and down the back of his head.

The paper wouldn't write itself, and he needed to finish the first draft tonight. The team had to leave tomorrow for a special afternoon staff meeting at Maranatha. Jeremy appreciated all the experience the ministry team gave him, but it wasn't easy being on the road every weekend and still keeping up with his studies.

"The seminary demands a lot from its students," Pastor Pete had warned him during his stopover in Greenlawn last summer. "They take their job of preparing you for future service very seriously. But don't be afraid to talk to the professors if there's a problem. And remember, you're preparing for the Lord's service. Give Him your time now, when you don't have a family, or other distractions. Put Him first. He'll provide what you need when you need it."

His problem didn't involve his professors. Jeremy brought up his online Bible program and found Psalm 37, verses 4 and 5.

"Delight yourself also in the LORD, and He shall give you the desires of your heart. Commit your way to the LORD, trust also in Him, and He shall bring it to pass."

These verses became his prayer. He had to stay focused and wait.

Before going to bed, Jeremy finished his first draft, then left another text message for Aubrey.

For more than an hour, he lay awake in his bed. When his eyes became heavy enough and his mind stopped spinning, he fell asleep.

WITH NO SCHEDULE TO keep for the day, Aubrey awoke later than normal on Saturday morning. She welcomed a day like this and listened to neighborhood sounds outside her window: the barking of dogs, car doors slamming, the laughter of children at play. For a few more minutes, she snuggled under her blankets.

Sweetie Pie blinked sleepy eyes at her when she picked up her cell phone from her nightstand and turned it on. She found Jeremy's text messages, to which she hadn't responded yesterday. Still fuming inwardly about his absence from the play performance Thursday, she wouldn't mention it. It obviously hadn't been as important to him as it was to her.

She texted him back, telling him her plans for the day to do as little as possible, with no explanation on why she didn't answer his messages and calls yesterday. She didn't tell him she missed him, although she did.

Stroking the cat cuddled against her side, she lay back on her bed. She hadn't meant to hurt Jeremy when she'd refused to go to Wellsburg with him next weekend. Maybe she should go, just to have time with him. And to visit with the Abbott family.

No. Haleigh had visited her at home after the accident five years ago, when Aubrey was still on crutches and going through painful physical therapy. The visit ended when Haleigh ran out of the house, angry and in tears.

Haleigh hadn't come back, and she rebuffed any efforts Aubrey made to renew the friendship, even after the Abbotts moved to Wellsburg. After that, when her family visited Greenlawn, she hadn't come with them, hadn't answered letters or responded to emails.

Aubrey didn't want to ruin the Abbotts' birthday celebration for Haleigh. She couldn't come between Jeremy and his sister. Maybe it would be better for her and Jeremy to give each other space right now.

After breakfast, she put on her coat and picked up her purse to go to the mall. Although she wouldn't exactly be alone there, she wouldn't have to carry on a conversation, explain anything, give any instructions, or listen to any whining students or demanding parents. She needed some time by herself, to think.

Her mother sat the kitchen table with a box of greeting cards.

"I'm going to the mall, Mom." Aubrey went to the back door and rested her hand on the knob. "Is there anything you need from there?"

"No, I can't think of anything." Mom looked up. "Are you going by yourself?"

"Yes. I'll be home in time for lunch."

"Okay. We'll just have soup and sandwiches. Our Saturday schedules are all different, so I don't plan meals like I do the rest of the week. Enjoy yourself."

She ignored the urge to talk to her mother about Jeremy, couldn't discuss this deeply personal heart trouble with Mom right now. She didn't know how to explain, and she might cry.

"Thanks, Mom, see you later." She closed the door behind her and got into her car.

Wandering in and out of the stores, Aubrey bought a few personal items as well as a few inexpensive things to use in the classroom. Christmas displays had already been set up, although Thanksgiving had not yet arrived. She spoke briefly to several acquaintances she met, answering questions about school and her plans for the future.

She strolled around Dunn's Department Store and browsed

through the dishes and linens in housewares, considering what patterns and colors she might choose for her own home. That led her thoughts back to Jeremy and their faltering relationship.

Had she been wrong to refuse to go with him to Wellsburg next weekend? Was it Haleigh's discomfort she was considering, or her own?

Though Jeremy meant well, she wouldn't force herself on Haleigh. If the invitation had come from Haleigh herself, she may have agreed to go. However, by refusing to go, she'd also refused time with Jeremy, something they both wanted. She'd hurt him. Would he forgive her?

She'd never second-guessed herself in this way. With a sigh she sat down on the wall enclosing the fountain in the center of the mall. Aubrey didn't like being unsure about something so important.

"This is sort of like old times, isn't it?" Several reusable, cloth shopping bags landed on the floor as a body moved in beside her.

Aubrey looked up. "Oh, hi, Katie!" Although she'd come to the mall to be alone, her friend's presence comforted her. Katie had a way of brightening a cloudy day.

"I didn't expect to meet you here this weekend." Katie pressed her palms against the seat and hunched her shoulders. "This is a nice surprise."

"The school where I teach has a four-day weekend, so I came home yesterday, and I'll go back on Monday." Aubrey shrugged. "This is only the second time I've come home this semester." She shifted to face her friend. "You must be almost finished."

"Yes, I'll graduate just before Christmas." She wrinkled her nose. "I still have to pass the state boards. I never did like tests."

"I'm sure you'll do fine." Aubrey put out her hand to catch the spray from the fountain.

Katie laid her hand on Aubrey's knee. Her green eyes expressed concern. "Is something wrong, Aubrey? You looked rather glum sitting here by yourself."

"I'm okay. I just have a few things on my mind." As close

friends, she and Haleigh and Katie had learned to read each other.

"Let's see ... school, or the future, or romance?"

"A little of each, I guess." Aubrey sighed, then straightened. "I like teaching. In fact, I talked with my advisor yesterday about getting a master's degree in special ed."

"That sounds interesting and challenging. You always liked a challenge."

"I have a boy in my class, a sweet boy, who has some physical and learning challenges. His smile makes my day, and he loves to learn. He's my inspiration. And the university women's track team helps special needs athletes."

"Do you see much of Jeremy Abbott? He's at Clark Seminary, right?"

Aubrey's shoulders slumped. "He's there, but I don't see much of him." She splayed her right hand, palm up. "I'm gone most of the week student teaching." She held up her left hand. "And he's gone on weekends with his ministry team." She clasped her hands together. "So, we squeeze in a run once in a while, or meet for a meal."

"You sound disappointed." Katie twisted a curl around her finger.

"You and I have both been friends with Jeremy for a long time. I always thought of him as a brother. When he told me he'd be at Clark Seminary, I thought what fun it would be to have him almost next door again."

"But ... ?"

"Since Mike's wedding, I've seen him in a different light."

"Which is ... ?"

"I told him I want to remain friends only, but I sometimes think of him as more than a friend. I really enjoy being with him."

"Aubrey." Katie tapped her lips with her finger. "My grandma has a book by Elisabeth Elliot. I read it while ... when I stayed at her house back when I was ... pregnant." Aubrey laid her hand on her friend's arm to encourage her. Katie continued. "Do you know who Elisabeth Elliot was?"

Aubrey thought for a moment. "Her husband, Jim, was killed on the mission field, right? I remember my parents talking about it, but it happened before they were born."

"Right." Katie nodded. "Well, in this book she writes about having to wait to marry Jim. He was very focused on what God wanted him to do: go to the mission field. So they waited, prepared to serve God, and God eventually brought them together in an amazing way."

"We haven't talked about the direction of our relationship or discussed getting married." Aubrey stared at her hands in her lap.

Had she lost sight of her goals? Like a runner who looks over her shoulder to see who's close behind her, was she getting off track and losing momentum? "Well, Jeremy has a year and a half of seminary left, and I have grad school next year. Maybe you're right, Katie. I have to stay focused."

The fountain spray felt cool and wet against her outstretched hand. "I invited him to the school play that I helped direct, but he didn't show up or let me know he wasn't coming. He may not want to see me again."

Katie's eyebrows went up. "What do you mean, not want to see you again?"

"He's going home next weekend for Haleigh's birthday."

"She'll be twenty-one."

"He asked me to go with him, and I said no." Aubrey gathered her hair and pulled it over her shoulder.

"Why?" Katie frowned.

"Haleigh hasn't spoken to me for five years. It's her special day, and it would ruin her birthday if I showed up unexpectedly. I couldn't do that to her, Katie." Or was her decision a ploy to protect herself from Haleigh's rejection?

"I understand what you're saying. Haleigh won't have anything to do with me, either."

"I'm not sure Jeremy understands, however. It upset him

when I refused to go with him. Of course, it doesn't help that we usually talk on the phone rather than face to face. Time together isn't a priority right now."

"I don't have any answers, girlfriend, except to say wait and see what happens. Focus on what you have to do now. And pray." Katie shook her head and played with one of her curls.

"Thank you for listening to me." Aubrey smiled and reached over to squeeze Katie's hand. "You've helped by letting me vent. Now, do you have plans for lunch, or can you come home with me? Mom's having soup and sandwiches, and I know she'd be glad to see you."

"You know, I'd like that." Katie smiled. "It's been a long time since I last ate at your house. It will be great to visit with your family again. I'm scheduled to work at the Senior Home later."

Aubrey grabbed her bags and stood, then left the mall with her friend, her heart lighter.

10

*T*he ministry team members took turns driving as they traveled together each weekend. This weekend they rode in Renée's car, with Sarah in the front seat while Renée drove. Jeremy sat in back with Kyle.

Jeremy heard chatter around him, but he paid little attention as he looked out the window, not seeing the passing scenery. The recent disagreement with Aubrey played over and over in his mind. A nudge to his side made him jump.

"Where are you, man?" Kyle asked. "You haven't heard a word of our conversation. We decided to open the door and leave you at the side of the road."

"Sorry, just thinking." Jeremy sat up straight and smiled at the teasing.

"Must be about a girl. Aubrey break up with you?"

He'd introduced Aubrey to Kyle but not to the two women. Jeremy shook his head.

"Is Aubrey the tall blonde you run with?" Sarah, a pretty seminarian with short, dark curls, looked at him over her shoulder.

"Yes." Jeremy brushed at the hair on his forehead. "When we get the time." How did she know Aubrey ran with him?

"Time? What's that?" Renée looked at him in the rearview mirror. "You don't talk about her much, Jeremy."

Why didn't he talk about her? He frowned thoughtfully.

At first the team had spent most of their time talking about classes and plans for their ministry. Then they'd opened up a little about personal matters.

Renée's fiancé worked on the mission field, Kyle had a serious relationship with a girl he'd met in college, and Sarah was unattached but interested in meeting the man of her dreams. He'd told them about Aubrey, but as the semester progressed and he and Aubrey found so little time together, he hadn't said much more about her.

"Aubrey's doing her student teaching this semester. Our schedules don't coincide. She's gone during the week, and I'm busy on weekends."

"Have you known her long?" Sarah shifted to peer at him between the front seats.

"We grew up together. She and my sister were friends, and our families spent a lot of time together. Then my family moved away from Greenlawn. We reconnected at her brother's wedding during the summer."

"As deaf as you were to us, I'd say you've got it bad, man." Kyle pushed on his shoulder.

Jeremy shrugged. His relationship with Aubrey was at a low point, and he didn't want to talk about her with the ministry team. He'd wait to talk to Jason next weekend. Maybe he could talk Haleigh into reconciling with Aubrey.

"My fiancé is on the mission field, and I haven't seen him in six months." Renée's statement caught his attention.

He met her glance in the rearview mirror.

"When are you getting married?" Sarah asked.

"Next spring, after I graduate. He'll come home, we'll get married, then we'll have six months or more to raise support."

"What does he do?" Jeremy watched Renée's face reflected in the mirror.

"Church planting. He's working right now with a team in Guatemala."

"My twin and his wife are considering church planting. How...?"

"How long have you been engaged?" Sarah asked the question before Jeremy could finish.

Renée sighed. "By the time I finish at Clark Seminary, it will be two years. I met him when he was on deputation, raising his support. We decided I should finish seminary before getting married, so he had to go without me."

"A long wait. It must take focus and determination." Kyle spoke Jeremy's thoughts out loud.

"Yes, and an act of obedience to God. Waiting isn't the worst thing in the world, but it's difficult."

"I guess we don't always get our way, even when we think we're right." Jeremy hadn't intended to say that out loud.

"You learn that God's way is best." Renée smiled.

Renée's words encouraged him, planted hope within him. If Renée and her fiancé could maintain a long-distance engagement, he and Aubrey could solve their problem. He'd have to find a few minutes to share the verses from Psalm 37 with her.

Time to get to work and get his mind off his problem. "So, what's happening tonight? Does anyone have a copy of the schedule?" They often used travel time to prepare for the weekend.

The unusual Saturday staff meeting would be followed by a church family night, beginning with a dinner at six. Maranatha was a growing church with new ministry opportunities, and Jeremy was excited to be a part of it, if only for a few weeks.

A COVERED DISH church family dinner followed the Sunday morning worship at Greenlawn Bible Church.

The brief respite from White Mountain Elementary School

and Clark University meant a break in Aubrey's busy schedule and time to enjoy being with family and friends. However, intruding thoughts of Jeremy made her restless and distracted. Their disagreement lay heavily on her mind and invaded her dreams at night.

She remained firm in her resolve not to go to Wellsburg, but she kept hearing the disappointment in Jeremy's voice.

For the last five years, she'd believed that one day she would reestablish her relationship with Jeremy's sister. That day had now become a necessity, for Jeremy's sake, if she hoped for a future with him. But Haleigh's twenty-first birthday party wasn't the right time or place. Was it?

Time after time she tried to bury the thought that she was afraid to confront Haleigh head-on. Afraid of rejection, of failure.

Life had become more complicated when she'd begun to think of Jeremy as more than a friend.

On Monday morning she walked to Floral Creations. A talk alone with Willie would be just the thing to help clear her perspective. Besides, she hadn't seen his finished shop yet.

A bell over the door jingled as she entered. She met her brother as he came from the back room carrying a flat of mums.

"Hey, Aubrey." He set the plants on the floor.

"Wow, Wills, I'm impressed. I saw your plans, but the whole layout is fantastic!" She walked through, admiring the gleaming wood paneling, the neat shelves and displays, Willie's office, and the greenhouse.

With his hands on his hips, he smiled as he gazed around, then back at her. "Thanks, Sis. It's been a lot of hard work, but certainly worth the effort. My business is picking up. Mom and Jesse come in to help sometimes, and I've hired a part-time college student." He wiped his hand across the counter. "I'm providing flowers for my first wedding next weekend, and I have several others lined up during the winter and spring."

Willie obviously loved his work, and the many hours he spent building his business seemed to energize him.

Aubrey lifted a pot and added it to Willie's display of mums and Thanksgiving arrangements.

"So, how's your love life?" He asked her the same question whenever she returned home, a sort of joke between them.

"Not very good at the moment." She shook her head and grimaced.

"Isn't Jeremy at the seminary? Or are you referring to someone else?"

"No, it's Jeremy." She sighed. "He lives the equivalent of a couple of blocks away, but we can't find time to see each other."

"What's the problem?" He handed her an arrangement and indicated where to place it.

"Life. School. Commitments. I'm student teaching, he's on a ministry team. I'm gone during the week, he's gone on weekends. And even when we're both there, he has hours of reading and writing, as well as classes. We argue when we talk. I'm wondering if our relationship will ever go anywhere."

Willie twisted his mouth and nodded as he lifted two plants from a flat. "That's tough. It's harder than you expected."

"Jeremy's going home next weekend for Haleigh's twenty-first birthday." She set a pot of rust-colored mums on a shelf and brushed her hands together to remove dirt.

"I remember the date." He set the two plants on the floor next to some pumpkins.

Of her three brothers, Willie was the most sensitive and caring, always willing to go out of his way to help people. He treated girls and women with respect, and she'd seen many feminine eyes following him. Mike always had a girlfriend during high school, and Jesse could be defined as girl crazy. But Willie?

Her brother still cared for Haleigh Abbott and still wanted to open communication with her, but he couldn't wait for her forever. When would he act on his feelings for Haleigh?

Aubrey didn't understand Haleigh's avoidance either. Maybe

fear kept her away. Fear of what? She didn't know. Haleigh couldn't still be holding on to her anger at Aubrey and Katie after five years, could she? Since Haleigh refused to talk to anyone about it, Aubrey might never know.

No, she wouldn't tell Willie about her refusal to accompany Jeremy next weekend. He probably wouldn't understand any better than Jeremy did.

Yet Willie hadn't made a further attempt to reconcile with Haleigh either. Or if he had, she didn't know about it. Five years was a long time to wait.

Neither of them, it seemed, was willing to confront Haleigh.

Aubrey helped Willie finish setting up the display and stepped back. "Looks good. I have to pack and have lunch before I leave."

"Thanks for your help. I'll have to hire you to be my assistant."

Although she and Willie hadn't talked through her problem with Jeremy, talking to him about Jeremy helped. She gave him a hug and left the shop.

She wanted to be back on campus before supper and had a few things to prepare for school tomorrow. Maybe she'd even have time to see Jeremy this evening.

The sun had just sunk below the horizon, darkness closing in quickly, when Jeremy stopped his car in the driveway in Wellsburg on Friday evening. Jason came out the front door and down the steps.

Jeremy got out of his car. "Hey, Bro', good to see you." It was their first meeting since the wedding in August.

"Same here." They greeted one another with a handshake and a slap on the back. "You didn't convince Aubrey to come."

"She was sure that Haleigh's birthday would be ruined if she came." Jeremy ran his hand through his hair.

"I think our little sister needs to know how her attitude is affecting all of us." Jason frowned and shook his head. "It's like she's boxed herself in. After five years, she should get over it. It seems to me she's carrying her hurt feelings too far."

"The problem is, she won't listen if we talk to her. She's so stubborn." Jeremy opened the back door of his car. "But then, so is Aubrey."

"Sometimes I can't figure my wife out." Jason grinned. "But Carmella complains about me at times, so I think the feeling is mutual."

Jeremy grabbed his suitcase and laptop from the back seat of his car, and the brothers entered the house. In the kitchen, his mother and sister-in-law were cleaning up after the evening meal. No, Haleigh wasn't there. Jeremy's heart sank.

"Hi, Mom." He set down his suitcase and laptop to enfold his mother in his arms.

"Glad you're home safely, Jeremy."

"Hey, Jeremy, it's good to see you." Carmella greeted him with a smile.

"Hi, Carmella. Are you making my brother behave?" Jeremy gave her a kiss on the cheek.

"I'm doin' my best."

Jeremy looked around. "Where's Haleigh?"

"They're having a party at the nursing home this evening." His mother opened the refrigerator to put away leftovers. "Haleigh and Sunshine were invited."

"But she will be here for her party tomorrow?" Jeremy cringed at the sarcasm in his tone. He didn't want Mom to think he intended disrespect for her.

"Of course, she'll be here." Mom gave him a reproachful look. "It's her birthday."

"I know, Mom. It's just ..." Jeremy shook his head and left his thought unfinished. "Is Dad in the living room?" He picked up his suitcase and laptop.

"Yes, he's watching the news."

Jeremy walked into the living room. "Hi, Dad."

"Good to see you, son." His father stood, and they embraced. "The news is almost over."

"I'll put my things upstairs and be back."

When he left for college, Jeremy had stored most of his possessions in the attic, although a shelf of sports trophies hung on the wall, and a photo of the Abbott family stood on the dresser. The familiar spread on the bed and curtains at the windows still identified this room as his.

The room had been rearranged to accommodate the twin bed from Jason's former room, which was now the guest room with a full-size bed. He placed his suitcase and computer on the extra bed and sat down. Taking a deep breath and releasing it slowly, he consciously relaxed his muscles.

It was good to be home. The busyness and stress of the semester had taken their toll. If only Aubrey had come with him, the weekend would be perfect.

By the time he returned to the living room, the rest of the family, except Haleigh, had gathered there.

"Can I get you anything to eat, Jeremy?"

"No thanks, Mom. I stopped and picked up something on the way. I'm good."

He and Jason got into a discussion about seminary experiences. Carmella talked about her job as the administrative assistant for a seminary professor. Jeremy concluded that their marriage thrived, although with bumps along the way. Mom and Dad caught them up on extended family news. Mom looked forward to having her family, the Harts, here for Thanksgiving this year.

The front door opened. Haleigh and Sunshine entered. "Hey, Jeremy, it's good to see you."

"You, too, Haleigh." Jeremy stood to greet his sister with a hug.

Quivering with delight, Sunshine moved from person to person, swishing her tail and begging for attention with her eyes.

Was Haleigh as happy as she seemed? Jeremy watched his sister. Did she have regrets about Aubrey? Would it make a difference if she knew how much her attitude affected him? He shook his head. He doubted it.

He settled in for several hands of Dutch Blitz with his brother, sister, and sister-in-law.

With Carmella's encouragement, Jason agreed to get up early to go for a run with Jeremy before breakfast.

"I'll be sure to give that sister-in-law of mine a big hug for this." Jeremy began his warm-ups.

"Carmella knows you and I have a lot of catching up to do." Jason paused with his hands on his hips. "And she understands that, as twins, we have a special bond. She's great!"

"Sounds like the honeymoon is still on." Jeremy grinned.

Jason stretched his calf muscles. "For the most part. We have our moments, however. Marriage makes you learn a whole lot about yourself that you didn't know before. Some of it not so good."

"I've heard that."

As usual, Jeremy fell into step with his twin. Their breath came out in white puffs in the crisp morning air. Lights shone from windows in a few houses. Their stomachs growled as the aroma of bacon and coffee wafted in the cold air. A neighbor's dog behind an electronic fence barked at them, breaking into the quiet of the morning.

"Shhh!" Jason hissed. "You'll wake up the neighbors!"

The dog stopped barking, wagged his tail, and lay on the ground with a whine.

"You've got the touch for sure. Even the dogs obey you." Jason chuckled at Jeremy's words.

"You said Aubrey wouldn't come because she didn't want to ruin Haleigh's day."

"That's what she said, anyway." Jeremy gestured with his hands.

"Well, knowing Aubrey, she said what she meant. How are you two getting along?"

"You know, Jase, I'm not really sure. I mean, last summer I thought we were on track for a permanent relationship."

"And now?"

Jeremy shook his head. "I don't know."

"What's the problem?"

"Even though I didn't choose Clark Seminary because Aubrey attended the university, I thought that going to Clark was a good idea, that we'd see each other every day. But since she started student teaching, and I started going away every weekend, we hardly find time to meet to say hello. We text, and when we talk on the phone, we end up arguing. It's so frustrating."

"That's tough, man."

"Yeah. I feel like God is pulling us away from each other. Seminary classes are more time-consuming than undergraduate work. I have to focus on classes and papers and the ministry team. And she's a White, focused on her goals, teaching, grad school next year."

"All the White kids are that way." Jason nodded. "Look at how successful Willie is already. He finished college early and went right into business."

They turned a corner and increased their speed, still in step.

"We both feel we're following God's leading in our education and preparation for the future." He blew out a breath. "I love her, Jase. I thought you were crazy to get married and go to seminary, but now I'm thinking you're the smart one. At least you can go home and be with Carmella at night."

Jason glanced at his twin. "You know, neither one of us regrets the decision to get married when we did. We don't have a lot of leisure time together, and we run on a pretty tight budget, but we're doing okay. God is good to us."

"Maybe it's time for me to take the next step forward." Was he crazy? His heart said no, he wasn't crazy, that it was time. His head said yes, but Aubrey wouldn't agree.

"Look, Jer. Just because I'm married now doesn't mean it's what God has in mind for you. Waiting is okay if you and Aubrey aren't ready."

"I know." Jeremy swiped his hair with his fingers. "I don't understand why God threw Aubrey into my path when He did, when neither of us looked for or expected love."

"Maybe it's a test to find out if you're really committed to the path He's laid out for you."

"I've thought of that. Keeping up with my studies while I work on building a relationship with Aubrey has been a challenge. Just when I thought we were making progress, everything became complicated. I thought we might be ready to talk about marriage during Christmas break, but now I don't know. It's like I've hit a roadblock, and my heart is looking for a detour."

"Then maybe it's just not your time, no matter how great your desire."

"Does Carmella mind having to work to put you through seminary?" Jeremy picked up speed and puffed as he talked.

"Why don't you ask her. She can give you a wife's perspective."

"And then there's Haleigh."

"I think, Jer, you're going to have to confront her. In the end, she'll be the loser if she doesn't make things right with Aubrey."

"I know."

Jeremy kept pace with his twin as they broke into a run.

The morning air held a definite autumn chill, but the sunrise turned the horizon pink and orange as Jeremy and his brother finished their run and returned to the house. The rest of the family were up. Sunshine greeted them with a happy "woof" and a zealously wagging tail as she came up to them for a pat. They crouched down, and she rolled over for a belly-rub.

"Did you have a good run?" Carmella entered the kitchen.

"The best." Jason rose to kiss his wife. "I'm going to shower, and I'll be back down for breakfast."

Haleigh stood in front of the stove.

Jason sniffed. "Are those pancakes you're making, Haleigh?"

"Blueberry pancakes, and real maple syrup." Haleigh looked over her shoulder with a pancake turner in her hand.

"What is this, a party or something?" He put his arm around Carmella.

"A party? Are we having a party?" Jeremy, still on the floor with the dog, looked up.

"Must be." Jason shrugged. "I saw a cake on the dining room buffet. It said, 'Happy 21ˢᵗ Birthday, Haleigh,'"

"Haleigh's having a birthday? And she's reached her majority?" Jeremy and his twin often finished each other's thoughts or ran a commentary together.

"But she's still just a squ…Ow!" Jason didn't get to finish saying 'squirt" before Haleigh slapped his arm with the pancake turner.

Sunshine got into the action now, barking and prancing.

"It's okay, Sunshine." Haleigh snapped her fingers. Sunshine stopped barking and sat next to her mistress.

Mom had been quietly watching her family as she set the table. She smiled at their antics, obviously loving having her family together.

"Ow!" Jason held his arm. "Mom, Haleigh hit me with the pancake turner!"

"Sorry, Jason, you should know better than to tease Haleigh about her size."

"Carmella?" He whined, looking at his wife with a woebegone expression.

She shook her head and held up her hands. "Far be it from me to get mixed up in a family squabble."

"Oh! The pancakes!" Haleigh turned to rescue the blueberry delicacies. "These will be for Jason." She placed the golden pancakes on a warm platter and covered them with foil.

"At least I know better than to bring Haleigh's wrath down on me. Especially on her twenty-first birthday. Happy birthday, Sis." Jeremy gave her a kiss on the cheek. He'd missed this playful interaction with his sister. Maybe today Haleigh would listen to him.

"Happy birthday, Sis," Jason kissed her other cheek.

"What a family!" Carmella gave her sister-in-law a hug.

"Thanks guys," Haleigh smiled at them. "The pancakes are nearly ready. Is Dad up?" She looked at Mom.

Mom nodded, but at that moment Dad entered the kitchen.

"Did I hear my name along with pancakes? Of course, I'm up, daughter. I was listening to the news."

Jason and Jeremy hurried upstairs to take quick showers.

A few minutes later, Jeremy joined his family as they sat down at the table in the homey kitchen. He bowed his head and tried to focus on Dad's prayer.

"Father in heaven, we come to you with praise in our hearts for this day and for our family gathering. Thank you for all our children, but today especially for Haleigh. Bless her day with special joy. And thank you for our breakfast, and for all your provisions for us. In Jesus' name, Amen."

"Amen," echoed around the table.

As they ate and talked, Jeremy looked at each member of his family. They lacked one person to make it complete: Aubrey.

Haleigh appeared quite happy and chatty today. He had to find a way to bring reconciliation between the two young women he loved best in the world.

After Jeremy and Jason washed and put away the breakfast dishes, Haleigh slipped on her boots and grabbed her coat. "Sunshine and I need some exercise. Anybody want to go for a walk with us?"

"The roast is in the oven, and dinner will be served at one, so I'd like to go with you," Mom said.

"Since it's a holiday of sorts, I think I'll join you." Dad shrugged into his coat and helped Mom with hers.

Jeremy zippered his coat and drew on his gloves. Sunshine quivered with excitement as Haleigh snapped the leash to the dog's collar. Jason helped Carmella with her coat.

As they all trooped out of the house, Dad and Jason walked together, Carmella paired up with Haleigh and her dog, and Jeremy walked with his mother.

Mom linked her arm with Jeremy's. "Is there something bothering you, Jeremy?"

"You know me well, Mom." Jeremy nodded.

"That's what mothers do. Do you want to talk about it?"

"I asked Aubrey to come with me this weekend." Jeremy sighed and swiped his hand through his hair.

"But she's not here."

"No, she's not. We've been trying to find time together since school started. With one thing and another, we've hardly seen each other, even though we live across campus from each other. I came up with the brilliant idea that, if she came with me, we would finally have the time to work things out. But she refused to come."

"Hmm. I suppose she had a reason for refusing."

"Haleigh."

Mom's raised eyebrows indicated her surprise.

"She said she didn't want to spoil Haleigh's birthday. That Haleigh hadn't spoken to her for five years and probably wouldn't like it if she showed up here this weekend."

This time his mother sighed. "I'm sorry, Jeremy. Your father and I have tried to get Haleigh to talk about the problem, but she refuses to deal with it. She hides it well, but she managed to find excuses not to go with us back to Greenlawn and we let her have her way. I don't know, but I think she may be holding on to some kind of shame or guilt. She's chosen to build a wall with the past."

Maybe Mom and Dad should have forced Haleigh to return to Greenlawn. "It's not fair, Mom. They used to be such good friends. We all had good times together." He spread out his arms. "Why can't she grow up and get over it?"

"You're both adults now, Jeremy. I'd hate to think of anything like this coming between you. Why don't you try to talk with Haleigh?"

"Do you think she'll listen?"

She studied his face. "This is really important to you, isn't it?"

"Yeah, Mom." He nodded. "I want to marry Aubrey."

"I thought there might be something serious developing between you two." She paused a moment and smiled. "Jim and

Annette's children used to be like our own. The idea of Aubrey as a daughter-in-law gives me joy." She patted his arm.

He smiled, glad for her support.

"I think you'll have to try, Jeremy. You've always been close to Haleigh. Maybe you can help her where we've failed. Maybe she'll make an effort to reconcile if she sees what it means to you."

"Thanks, Mom. That's what I'm hoping as well." His heart felt lighter after this unplanned talk with Mom. Now, to find the right moment to approach Haleigh.

"And you know your dad and I will be praying."

"I know, Mom. I guess there wouldn't be much hope without God's help."

When Dad dropped back to walk next to Mom, Carmella moved up beside Jason. Jeremy watched his sister ahead of him with her dog. Maybe it was time.

Dad took Mom's hand. "I think I'm ready to go in, Libby. We'll let the young people go on."

Always an active man who loved sports as much as his sons, it troubled Jeremy to see his father tired and winded after such a short time. Maybe it was the cold air. Probably he'd been working too hard lately.

"All right, dear." She squeezed Jeremy's hand and took her husband's arm. "I've got some things to do for dinner anyway."

Jeremy knew that Mom would probably share their discussion with Dad, but that was all right. He needed both his parents praying for him. As they turned back, he jogged up beside his sister.

"I imagine Sunshine misses you when you're at school." Sunshine, hearing her name, wagged her tail.

"I'm home every weekend, at least most weekends." Haleigh patted Sunshine's head. "I wouldn't have much time to spend with her at school."

"Have you been going out with her often? To the hospital and nursing home, I mean."

"Most weekends we do something. One weekend we were invited to a birthday party for a little boy with cerebral palsy. And there's an elderly man who loves to have Sunshine visit him in the nursing home." She nodded. "We find plenty to do."

"Aubrey's thinking about getting her master's degree in special education. Some special needs kids have service dogs. Maybe you two should get together and talk about it."

Haleigh stiffened beside him and said nothing.

"I asked Aubrey to come this weekend. But she refused."

She changed the position of the dog's leash in her hand. Her jaw tightened.

"She wouldn't come because she thought it would ruin your birthday party." He plunged in. "She doesn't think you want to see her."

Haleigh bit her lip. Her face reddened and tears filled her eyes.

"Aubrey and I have been seeing each other." Well, they did occasionally. "I plan to see more of her. Please, Haleigh, will you talk to her, make things right between the two of you?"

"I-I can't! What I did...it's been too long!" With a sob, she began to run, her dog staying with her. Sunshine bounced playfully, but Jeremy knew Haleigh wasn't playing.

"Haleigh, come back! I'm sorry!" Jeremy watched her as she passed Jason and Carmella and disappeared around the corner. Jeremy started after her but stopped when he came even with his brother and sister-in-law. "That went well."

"I guess she didn't want to talk." Jason shook his head. "I'm sorry, Jer, I thought you could reason with her."

"Do you want me to go after her, make sure she's okay?" Carmella took a step as though to follow Haleigh.

"No, it's between Haleigh and me. I don't understand her at all!"

"Don't give up, Jer." Jason laid a hand on Jeremy's back. "Maybe she's finally getting the message. I'm sure God would like to see this all straightened out."

"I know." Jeremy sighed. Hope disappeared with his sister's retreating figure.

Jeremy returned to the house with Jason and Carmella. Haleigh and Sunshine came in a little later, Haleigh's face composed, appearing unruffled. Tension that hadn't been there earlier permeated the house. Jeremy didn't know what to say to make it go away.

*A*ubrey took a deep breath and blew it out slowly as she closed her laptop. She stretched and pulled her hair away from her face, letting it fall against her back. Since Christina had joined Daniel to study at the library, she was alone in her dorm room.

Should she call Jeremy? She checked her cell phone for the tenth time and shook her head. No, they'd probably be in the middle of Haleigh's party, not a good time to disturb him.

The missed opportunity to be with Jeremy and talk to Haleigh nagged at her. Had she made a mistake when she refused to go with him? Would it have mattered to Haleigh if she'd been there? Her indecisiveness made her angry at herself. An unusual tension headache threatened. She took a deep breath and let it out slowly, releasing the tightness in her muscles.

Six months ago, her life's GPS had been set and her destination unquestioned. She hadn't experienced this much uncertainty about anything since her accident when she was sixteen.

Her phone rang. Jeremy. Aubrey laid her red pen on top of the pile of spelling tests she'd been correcting and let the ring tone sound a second time. Taking a deep breath, she clicked it on.

"Hi, Jeremy. Good timing. I got in just a few minutes ago."

"I missed you today." She detected sadness and strain in his voice. Or her own guilty feelings made it sound that way.

"How was the party?"

"It was good. A few relatives and friends came. And I enjoyed being together with my family."

Aubrey waited for him to say something about Haleigh. Instead, he asked, "How was your day?"

"Okay. Busy. Lonely." She licked her lips and continued. "I researched graduate schools on the Internet. I've decided to apply to a state university and a Christian university with degree programs in special ed."

"Oh, is this for next fall?"

Why did he sound surprised? He knew she planned to get her master's degree.

"I'm considering next summer if I can get in. But we'll have to see. I'm not sure yet."

"Oh. Well, I guess you'll have to act soon if you want to get in at all."

"I guess." Aubrey picked up her pen and tapped it against her desk, trying to decide what to say next, something that would ease the tension. A dog barked. Sunshine.

"What are you doing now?" Jeremy asked.

"Well, earlier I went for a run. I just got back from the Commons, where we had a rousing discussion about graduate schools. I'm correcting spelling tests now, or I was when you called." Although tempted, she refused to add, 'I miss you.'

"I'm sorry I interrupted."

"No, Jeremy, you don't have to apologize. I hoped you'd call. I thought of calling you but didn't want to interrupt the party."

"You did? I wasn't sure you'd want to talk to me."

She stiffened and forced herself to keep her voice even. "Of course I want to talk to you! Why would you think otherwise?"

"I guess when you refused to come with me, I had my doubts."

"I tried to explain why." She rolled the red pen around on the desk. "I suppose it sounded rather lame to you."

"It seemed like a golden opportunity to take care of two problems, but I guess it wasn't to be. Haleigh refused to talk to me about her relationship with you. She said she can't make things right."

His sad, discouraged tone prevented Aubrey from saying *I told you so.* The rift between her and Haleigh reinforced the wall between her and Jeremy.

What had happened to the flame that had sparked and flared between them not long ago? Would the dying embers ever be reignited?

After Jeremy's call, Aubrey finished the spelling tests and checked her lesson plans for next week. With Thanksgiving in two weeks, she had only three weeks of practice teaching remaining. After spending the last few days of the semester on campus, she'd go home for three weeks and celebrate Christmas and the New Year with her family.

Tomorrow afternoon she'd go online again to look over the application process for the two schools to which she wanted to apply.

That night, Aubrey shifted from her left side to her back to her right side in bed. Unless she and Jeremy could talk things out and find a solution, they were done. She had to know where she stood with him and what direction their relationship was going. Remaining single for life would be better than this emotional roller coaster.

She finally fell asleep in the early morning.

THAT EVENING, Jeremy played Scrabble with Jason, Carmella, and Haleigh.

"Jeremy, where are you tonight? If you had put your word here, you'd have a triple score." Haleigh pointed to the pink square.

"Oh, sorry." Jeremy shrugged.

"Yeah, where's your sense of competition, Jer?" Jason gave him a questioning look.

"Not here, obviously." Haleigh straightened a few of the letters on the board.

Jeremy got up abruptly, jiggling the Scrabble board. "I guess I'm done." He saw his sister's stricken look, but he didn't give her a chance to say anything else. Claustrophobia clawed at his insides, and he needed to get away from everybody. Grabbing his coat, he went out the front door.

The stars twinkled in the dark sky overhead as Jeremy walked around the block, his breath forming fog.

The phone wasn't enough. He and Aubrey had to find time soon to talk face-to-face. He couldn't stand this limbo. If they didn't have an honest and open talk, he'd lose her. His heart ached, wanting to share with her his hopes and dreams for their future together.

"Oh, no!" He stopped and slapped his forehead with the palm of his hand, then groaned. "What a fool! I promised Aubrey I'd go to her play, and I forgot! And it's taken me this long to remember! How could I do that?" Shaking his head, he continued his walk. He'd neglected to write the date in his calendar. No wonder Aubrey hadn't responded to his messages for so long.

He'd never had such a problem lining up his priorities before.

"Oh, no!" He laid his hand on top of his head. He hadn't told Aubrey he'd committed to take a mission's trip during Christmas break either. He stood on the dark street outside his family's home in Wellsburg, his hands fisted at his sides and tears rolling down his cheeks.

Tired and frustrated, he prayed, "God, what's Your plan? If the desires of my heart are not Your will, show me Your will.

Please. Show me what to do." He wiped away his tears with his fists, glad to hide his pain in the darkness that enshrouded the neighborhood.

Returning to the house, he didn't stop to talk to anyone.

"Jeremy!" Haleigh called out, as he started up the stairs.

He simply put up his hand to acknowledge her and continued to his room.

In the morning he left before his sister got up. He wanted plenty of time to prepare for his Sunday school class at Maranatha. In his present state of mind, he'd be good for nothing. Spending time alone in the prayer room this morning seemed like a good option.

By the time the rest of the team arrived at the church, Jeremy felt ready, although not entirely satisfied.

AUBREY RODE to church with Christina and Daniel. *Two's company, three's a crowd* kept coming to mind as she watched the couple. Jealousy lay around her neck like a noose. Christina had Daniel with her almost every day. Aubrey forced herself to pay attention to the service and not the people beside her.

"I know I shouldn't feel this way, Father." She prayed silently. "I'm sorry. I'm angry with Jeremy, jealous of Christina. I'm a mess, God. Please forgive me and give me Your peace. In Jesus' name."

Refocusing her heart and mind to worship God helped Aubrey set aside her bad thoughts for a while.

After dinner at the Commons, Aubrey returned with Christina to their room. She stared out the window, wondering how she'd spend the afternoon. If she stayed in, she'd go crazy with boredom and thinking about Jeremy. What could she do?

"Hey, Roomie."

Aubrey looked over her shoulder at Christina.

"Daniel has a guy thing to do this afternoon. Do you want to take a walk with me? We haven't had a lot of time together this semester, and it's time to catch up on the news."

"Sounds good to me." Aubrey almost hugged Christina. "I think I have everything set for school tomorrow, and I don't have any other plans for this afternoon."

The two young women put on their coats, not saying much as they walked down the stairs and out the door. Aubrey took a deep breath of the crisp air. Bare tree branches waved at them, and a brisk breeze blew dry leaves across their path. High, wispy clouds scooted across the blue sky.

"Wouldn't it be fun to rake up piles of leaves and jump in them?" Christina caught a single burgundy leaf that floated down in front of her.

"I was thinking the same thing." Aubrey stepped on some dry, brown leaves in her path. They crunched. "We had so much fun with leaves in the fall when we were kids."

Aubrey enjoyed the delightful rustling and crunching noises they made as they kicked the leaves in front of them. She allowed Christina to direct them along the sidewalks across campus to the edge of the seminary grounds, where Aubrey tried not to dwell on missing Jeremy. They turned up the hill toward the university prayer garden, a quiet place of meditation and prayer frequented by faculty and students alike.

Finding it already occupied, they continued on until they came to an arched bridge over a small pond. Picnic tables sat within a small grove of evergreen trees. During their years at Clark, the roommates had enjoyed many visits to this peaceful, restful spot on campus.

In silent, mutual consent, they headed for the tables. The trees offered some protection from the wind, and they sat on a bench, leaning their backs against the edge of the table.

For a few minutes Aubrey savored the quietness and peacefulness of her surroundings. She rested her elbows on the table behind her and closed her eyes. She'd been so busy this semester, she'd forgotten to come here.

"Okay, Aubrey."

Christina's voice broke into the peacefulness, and her eyes popped open. Next to her, Christina straddled the bench, watching her.

"I want to know what's going on with you and Jeremy. You hardly talk about him anymore, and you don't spend much time together. You look at your phone a lot, but you don't call him. And I don't think he's calling you very often. What's going on?"

She didn't cry often, but a couple of tears escaped down her cheeks, and she wiped them away with her gloved hand.

"I'm not sure." She sniffed and searched her pockets for a tissue.

"Did you have a fight?"

"Not exactly a fight, but a disagreement." Aubrey hesitated, unsure how much she wanted to tell Christina. She didn't take failure lightly, didn't want her friend to get the wrong impression of Jeremy's family, and didn't want to complain about Haleigh.

"Jeremy invited me to go home with him for his sister's birthday." She straightened her back and turned toward her companion. "And I said no."

"Because?"

"Because of his sister, Haleigh."

"Haleigh. Wasn't she one of the Three Sisters group you used to belong to?"

"We were best friends as kids." Aubrey nodded. "Haleigh, Katie, and I did everything together. We were close, like sisters." She pressed three fingers together. "Haleigh and I shared our brothers with each other and with Katie." She smiled briefly. "We thought we'd be best friends forever."

"What happened?" Christina swung one leg over the bench so she faced outward.

Aubrey bit the corner of her mouth. "I think it was life and growing up. Katie and I started doing things that didn't include Haleigh. We made new friends. I got into sports and Katie did drama. Haleigh wasn't interested in either one, so she decided we had rejected her friendship, and she's refused to communicate with us for five years, even though both of us attempted to reach out to her at first."

Her accident, Katie's pregnancy, and Haleigh's grandmother's death had happened at nearly the same time. Haleigh must have felt lost and alone. Maybe she truly believed her friends didn't care.

"Oh, I see." Christina blew on her hands. "That does make a sticky situation."

"You have to understand that the Abbotts and Whites have always been friends, so I wouldn't have minded visiting Jeremy's family. But Haleigh ... I didn't want to force myself on her for her birthday. I don't think Jeremy quite understood."

"He's giving you the silent treatment?"

"No, not that. It's just that we hardly get to talk, except on the phone, and we almost get into an argument every time. We don't have much time see each other, and I'm beginning to wonder whether we're meant to be together." She shivered and turned up the collar of her coat.

"And then ..." she took a deep breath, "Jeremy forgot his promise to come to the school play two weeks ago, and he hasn't said a word about it. I guess it wasn't important to him, so maybe I'm not important to him." She put her hands in her pockets.

Christina shook her head. "No, I've seen the way he looks at you and how he treats you when you're together. You're just as important to him as he is to you."

"Do you think so?" Aubrey felt a twinge of hope. "Have you and Daniel made any plans yet?" Maybe she could draw more hope from her friend.

"We've talked about marriage, although it's not official yet." Christina tucked her hands under her arms. "We'll wait a year after graduation so we can both work and start paying back school loans."

"At times I think my relationship with Jeremy will go

nowhere. Last night on the phone we could hardly think of anything to say." Or saying the wrong thing might start an argument.

Christina remained silent. Either she'd finished what she wanted to say, or she wanted Aubrey to come to her own conclusions.

"I'm going to apply for graduate school. If I get accepted, I'd like to start this summer. It may take a while to finish because I'll be teaching at the same time. Jeremy has another year of seminary anyway. I think it's time to return to plan A. I can't waste my time wondering." Aubrey crossed her arms in front of her, feeling chilled.

Christina shivered. "I don't know about you, but I'm getting cold. Are you ready to go back?"

"I am." Aubrey stood and stretched, more hopeful after their talk. "I think I'll go back to the dorm, wrap up in a blanket, and read for a while." She yawned. "And maybe take a Sunday afternoon nap." Her sleep had been brief last night.

Christina grimaced. "I have some compositions to grade. But I promise to be quiet so you can sleep."

Dark clouds had covered the sun. Aubrey hoped the snow would hold off for a few days longer, at least until she was safely in Greenlawn for Thanksgiving.

"Thank you, Christina, for listening to me. I needed someone."

"That's what friends are for."

As usual, Jeremy arrived back on campus late Sunday night. Because of his bad mood, he didn't call Aubrey or even text her.

The weekend at home had been a near disaster, not at all the problem-solving time he hoped for.

Although he'd managed to fulfill his responsibilities with the ministry team, he'd been out of sync with them today. In fact, his communication with God had been distant all weekend.

As he feared, his relationship with Aubrey distracted him from his purpose for being here. With only a few weeks left, finishing the semester well had to be his priority. He'd worked too hard to fail now.

The sooner he found time for Aubrey, to apologize to her and to talk, the better. He had to see her, to watch her face as they talked, to learn how she really felt about them.

In his sleep he saw her form in the mist ahead. When he called to her, she looked over her shoulder, smiled, and vanished in the mist.

On Monday morning, Aubrey found two envelopes tucked beneath the windshield, her name neatly typed on each one. She set her briefcase on the back seat, slid into the driver's seat, and started the car before trying to read them. Opening the one with a number 1 on it, she unfolded a sheet of paper with a large sad face and the words,

I'm sorry I missed your play.

Jeremy

She bit her lip. He finally remembered.

Opening the second envelope, she found a card printed on computer paper. A red rose adorned the front, and inside Aubrey read:

Dear Goldie,

Please have dinner with me on Wednesday. Unless I hear differently from you, I will pick you up at six. Afterward I'd like to take you to hear

a college choir concert. Renée said they're really good. I promise I won't keep you out late, but I'm hoping we'll be able to talk.

Love,
Jeremy

Thoughtfully, she slid the card back into the envelope.

Her windshield now clear, she put the car in gear, backed out of her parking space, and turned onto the street. She took a deep breath and released it slowly.

Unless she had a required meeting, she'd accept Jeremy's invitation. He obviously cared about her, and they needed time to talk. But for the present, she had to keep her mind on the traffic and her driving.

RENÉE HAD AGREED to put the notes on Aubrey's car Monday morning, for which Jeremy was thankful. A man lurking around the women's dorm in the early morning would have raised an alarm.

That night, Haleigh called him.

"Hi, Haleigh."

"Hi, Jeremy." She paused. "Thank you for coming home for my birthday."

"I always do."

"I know." She cleared her throat. "I apologize for what happened, what I said."

"Then you'll talk to Aubrey?" A spark of hope.

"No, I didn't mean that."

"Look, Haleigh, I don't know all that happened five years ago, but I think it's time for you to deal with it." His resentment flared. "You're my sister, and I'll always love you, but you're an adult, and I'm not going to tiptoe around you anymore."

"I'm sorry." Haleigh choked on her words. "Bye."

Jeremy inhaled and exhaled slowly after the tense conversation. He wouldn't let his sister keep him apart from Aubrey.

Excitement replaced some anxiety when Aubrey phoned him later on Monday night to say she would go out with him.

Next Sunday would be the last service date at Maranatha for the ministry team. He expected to finish the semester with good grades.

TRYING to release tension as he left to pick up Aubrey on Wednesday evening, Jeremy took a deep breath and blew it out. Tonight, he had time, although brief, to spend with her.

As he opened the car door for her, his heart beat faster. Her blue winter coat accentuated the blue of her eyes. He smiled and bowed playfully as she smiled back and slid gracefully into the seat. The tension hovered between them, but it seemed right for them to be together like this. He regretted all the time he'd missed with her.

They could get good food for a low price and quick service at the mall food court a short way from Clark. Although he'd rather have chosen a nice restaurant, his student budget wouldn't allow the expense. Aubrey understood that.

"First of all," he said as he seated her and then sat down across from her, "I want to apologize for missing your school play. I intended to go, but I—um—forgot. Sarah and I had a planning session for a team-taught Sunday School lesson."

She pressed her lips together when he said Sarah's name.

"I wondered." She positioned her plate in front of her. "I thought maybe it wasn't important to you, or maybe you were getting back at me because I wouldn't go to Wellsburg with you." Aubrey kept her voice even, but her blunt words crushed him.

"Do you think I'm that shallow?" His heart fell as he shook his head. "I really wanted you to go home with me, but I wouldn't take revenge. I thought you knew me better than that." This conversation was not going as he'd planned. "Of course, the play was important to me. You're important to me."

They said grace and began to eat. Tension laced the air between them.

"I've been thinking a lot about us."

"I have as well." He pushed his fork into a French fry. He'd been trying to figure the right time to propose to her. If he made his intentions clear, their relationship might get on the right track again.

"When Willie started his florist business, I told him it looked as though he had his life planned out." She leaned forward. "He reminded me that no matter what our plans are, it's God's plan that matters. We both know that God wants us to finish our education. I think we need to concentrate on our studies right now. Later we can concentrate on our relationship."

He choked on his food. He knew Aubrey well enough to know she had more to say, and he wasn't sure he liked the implication of her words so far.

"Are you all right?" she asked as he caught his breath.

He took a sip of cola, then nodded. "Yes. No! What do you mean?"

"We have only a few weeks until the end of the semester. We've been unsuccessful in spending much time together. Let's not even try for a while."

"But, Aubrey, I ..." He shook his head. "You want to break up with me?"

"I didn't think of it in those terms, but I guess, yes. At least for a while. To give us time."

"Time for what? This is about the play, isn't it? You're mad at me for missing it."

"No, Jer, it's not—"

"Then it's my sister." At that moment it was a good thing his sister was far away. He wanted to shake some sense into her.

She pushed her plate back. "No, not that. I just want us to

take some time apart until we're sure our relationship is God's will. We need some space. I don't want to be a distraction to you."

"And that's how you think of me, a distraction?" He'd thought of their relationship in the same terms, but to hear her say it upset him. "Aubrey, I care about you a lot. In fact, I know without a doubt that I l—

"No, Jeremy." She put up her hand. "Don't say it. Not now. Can't we just be friends for now?"

Jeremy stared at his food. As far as he was concerned, his relationship with Aubrey had developed beyond friendship. She obviously had doubts. To be honest, so did he.

Although they faced hurdles in their relationship, he hadn't believed she wanted to break up with him. He pinched the back of his hand under the table. Yes, this conversation was really happening.

"This is all wrong," he muttered. He checked his watch. "I think we'd better finish eating if we want to get to the concert on time." He looked at her. "That's if you still want to go." He couldn't think clearly enough to continue this discussion now.

"We should still go. I'd like to hear the choir. But I'm finished. I can't eat another bite."

Jeremy nodded and got up. He didn't feel like eating any more. Only illness made him lose his appetite, until now.

"Aren't you going to finish your meal?" She looked from the unfinished food to his face.

"I'm done." He tried to sound polite even through his anger. If they went to the concert, he'd have a little more time with her. If he could only think of a way to convince her that they belonged together.

During the concert, he tried to come up with an alternative to breaking up. He couldn't say much about the concert itself, although Aubrey said it was good.

When he walked her to the door of her dormitory later that evening, he still didn't know what to do. He'd failed to smooth things out between them. The tension felt like a rubber band about to snap.

"This will be best, Jeremy, for both of us. We agreed to be friends, and we don't have time to be more than that. I'm not sure God wants us to be more than friends ever. It's too distracting, and all we do is argue."

"I guess you've been considering a break-up for a while." He needed some time alone to pray before anything else. "All right, Aubrey, we'll do it your way."

She opened her mouth to speak.

"I won't change my mind." He cut her off. "But you take all the time you need."

"I'll be sending in my application for graduate school next week. I still want to be certified in special education."

He looked away from her for a moment and swallowed. "You know I won't stand in the way of your education goals." He'd thought of asking her to delay her goals, however.

"I know, Jeremy. It will just be better this way. Maybe we'll have time to get together during Christmas vacation."

His mouth formed an O, and he shook his head. "No, I'm leaving on a mission's trip a couple of days after Christmas. I won't be back until the day before the new semester begins."

"See what I mean." She frowned. "When were you planning to tell me?"

"When have I had the time?" he snapped.

She raised her eyebrows.

"Oh, Aubrey, I'm sorry." He lowered his voice. "I didn't mean to speak to you that way." He ran his fingers through his hair. "The plans for the trip were finalized only yesterday. I intended to tell you tonight, but other things—"

"I'd better go in." She took a step toward the door. "It was ... nice getting together with you tonight. Thanks for dinner. I'll see you around." She jerked open the door and hurried inside.

Jeremy stood frozen as he watched her go. He'd hurt her

feelings, but she'd crushed him with her rejection. At least no one else had been around to witness their scene.

This was crazy! How could he ever ask her to marry him when this might be the last time she spoke to him? They both needed time to cool off. He got into his car and drove to his apartment on the seminary campus, fighting the temptation to press hard on the accelerator.

Had romance turned into a battle of wills? Aubrey didn't like to lose. Would he have to concede?

He started an outline for the ministry report due next week, but his mind wandered.

From his desk he lifted the framed photo of Aubrey he took at Mike's wedding last summer. Her beauty and joy radiated from her sparkling eyes and smile. He loved it when she smiled like that. Tonight, there had been sparks, but no sparkle. The same beautiful face, but no joy. He set the photo down.

Longing to call his twin welled up. But Jason had his own life now. He could call his father, but he didn't feel quite desperate enough. He and Aubrey had to work this out themselves.

Loneliness, like a dark cloud, pressed in on him. He had an ethics paper due Friday, and he still had to finish preparing Sunday's lesson for a young adult class. Turning on his laptop, he stared at the screen without comprehension, then turned it off and pushed it aside.

With his hands covering his face, his elbows propped on his desk, he began to pray.

STOMACH ROILING, Aubrey ran up the stairs to her room. By the look on Jeremy's face, she didn't explain herself well. How could she speak more clearly when she didn't understand exactly what she wanted?

Why did she get so angry? What did it matter that he hadn't

told her about the missions trip? She was the one who wanted to break up, at least for a while.

But did she really?

She dropped her Bible and purse on her desk and shrugged her coat off her shoulders, not caring that it landed on the floor. She threw herself on her bed and burst into sobs. When did life become so crazy and out of control?

When Christina came in a few minutes later, Aubrey still lay on her bed.

"Are you okay?"

"No." She spoke into her pillow.

"I take it your time with Jeremy didn't go well."

"No."

The bed shifted as Christine sat on it. "Want to talk about it?"

"I think we're finished." She raised her head. "I'm not sure he'll ever talk to me again. I feel terrible."

"That bad?" The bed wiggled again. "What happened?"

Aubrey sat up. "I-I told him I thought we should stop seeing each other, not that we see each other often, so that we could pray about God's will for our lives. That we could be just friends for now."

"And ... ?" Christina handed her a tissue.

"He didn't take it too well." She wiped her tears. The awful look on his face had spoken volumes. "And when he tried to tell me he loved me, I stopped him. I wouldn't let him say it." She blew her nose.

Christina's eyes widened. "You're kidding! You two belong together, and you know it!"

"Then why don't we have time for each other?" Aubrey grabbed her pillow and hugged it to her. "Everything else is more important. He's so busy, and I've had practice teaching. We haven't had time to even run together, something we both like to do. When I have a weekend free, he's busy with his ministry team. And he can't even remember a promise." Aubrey shook her head.

"It seemed ideal for him to attend Clark Seminary." She paused, and when Christina didn't say anything, she added, "And when I suggested maybe we could see each other during Christmas break, he told me he'll be leaving on a missions trip two days after Christmas, and he won't be back until just before the start of next semester. I blew up at him."

"Because he's going on a missions trip?"

"No, because he waited until now to tell me." She wiped her tears with the back of her hand. When she said it out loud, she sounded like a spoiled brat. She prided herself on her maturity.

Christina stood and walked over to her desk, pulled out her chair, and sat facing Aubrey. From the stern look on her roommate's face, Aubrey prepared herself for a much-deserved lecture. It couldn't make her feel any worse than how she already felt.

"In the three and a half years I've known you, I've never seen you like this. First of all, I think you treated Jeremy shamefully."

Aubrey opened her mouth to defend herself.

"You'd already told him you wanted to stop seeing him when he told you about the trip. Why did you get angry? Was it because your plans didn't work out?"

"What do you mean?" Aubrey bit her lip.

"You're a good student and focused on what you're doing. You're good at working through challenges that come your way. You've willingly met the school's community service and other requirements. You've had admirers and dates, but this is the first time you've had a serious beau, and you have to think about him as well as yourself."

"Are you saying I'm selfish?" Aubrey frowned.

"Maybe a little." Christina shrugged. "When I started dating Daniel and we fell in love, I realized life became more complicated because I had to think about two people rather than one."

"And you think I got mad because I couldn't have my way."

Christina tipped her head. "Well?"

Selfish? Aubrey got up and walked to the window. Hadn't she always made herself available to help her friends and family?

Greenlawn High had emphasized community service. Her church and parents had encouraged service projects to help people in need and to support missionaries. Each semester at Clark until the present one, she'd joined Christina and other students in at least one university-sponsored service project. Each service project had given her satisfaction. Each one she ticked off as a goal achieved.

Until last summer, graduating from Clark and getting her master's degree had been her next goal. Now there was Jeremy. Had she relegated Jeremy and her desire to get married to another goal to be achieved?

She pulled down a slat of the blind and peeked out at the lawn behind the dorm, covered in dark shadows. Then she turned to face Christina. She didn't always agree with her roommate, but Christina never backed away when she had something to say. Usually, it was something Aubrey needed to hear.

"Maybe you're right. We Whites tend to pursue our goals until we reach them. My brother Willie finished four years of college in less than three and began his own florist business right away. Once he decided it was the right way, nothing stopped him. And his business is doing great." While she, a year older, hadn't graduated from college yet.

"Jeremy and I respect each other's goals." She pulled her hair over her shoulder. "He's preparing to be a preacher, and I plan to go on for my doctorate. We thought God's plan for us included spending time together this year. After all, we live the equivalent of four blocks from each other. But our schedules and career goals have interfered. I guess I took my frustration out on him."

"What will you do now?"

Aubrey sat on the corner of her bed and stared at the floor.

Her coat lay where she'd dropped it. "Oops! I guess I was a little upset when I came in." She picked up the coat and hung it in the closet, then faced Christina.

"I didn't begin to think seriously about marriage until last summer, when I saw Jeremy at Mike's wedding. I planned to go to graduate school before that. Time apart will be good for both of us." She wished she really believed her words. "Maybe my destiny is to remain single. If God intends for us to be together, He'll make a way."

Had she been trying to figure this out on her own? Had she even asked God for direction?

"I hope you and Jeremy work something out." Christina stood and put her chair back in place.

Aubrey tried to set aside her conflict with Jeremy as she finished correcting homework assignments and chose her outfit for tomorrow. Despite all she'd said about time apart being good for them both, she couldn't forget the shock on Jeremy's face when she'd left him at the door.

"By the way, are you busy Thanksgiving weekend?" Christina's question broke into the silence and her thoughts.

"Some of our extended family will be coming for Thanksgiving dinner on Thursday. Other than that, I plan to just spend time with my family." Without Jeremy.

"Well, Daniel's brother was able to get concert tickets for Saturday night, and we wondered if you wanted to come to the concert with us. We intended to invite Jeremy, too, but under the circumstances, I guess we'd better not. You can spend the weekend at my house and come back to school from there."

"It sounds good. Who's performing?"

As they discussed the concert and Thanksgiving weekend, her memory of the sadness in Jeremy's eyes tempered her excitement. The concert would be a perfect diversion. Maybe.

*P*eriods of wakefulness and dreams punctuated Aubrey's sleep that night. Driving to school the next morning, she kept the heat off and opened the window a crack.

She walked into the classroom yawning. Mrs. Breck paused while writing on the blackboard. "Are you feeling all right?"

Although they had a good professional relationship, Aubrey didn't discuss details of her personal life with Mrs. Breck.

"I didn't sleep much. A lot on my mind." Aubrey hung her coat in the closet and locked her purse in the desk drawer. "I'll have to keep busy, so I don't fall asleep."

As the day progressed and she became involved with the students, Aubrey's brain fuzziness wore off.

Mandy and Greg worked together planning games for their class's First Thanksgiving commemoration. Seated side by side, they shared a book from Mrs. Breck's personal library.

"It's amazing to watch Mandy and Greg, isn't it?" Mrs. Breck stopped beside her.

"You'd never know they had problems a few weeks ago."

"Mandy's parents met with me. I think our frank talk with Mr. Stevens helped him to see his responsibility in the matter."

"Your calmness helped him to relax."

"Yes. I've learned that parents usually want to protect their children, so if I remain calm, the situation isn't as apt to explode."

Aubrey nodded. "There's a verse in the Bible that says a gentle answer turns away anger. I think it's in Proverbs." Too bad she hadn't remembered that verse last night.

"Wise words."

A student raised his hand, and Mrs. Breck went to talk to him.

Greg looked up and smiled at Aubrey, and her heart went out to him. She looked forward to teaching more kids like Greg. Now she had to concentrate on finishing her student teaching and the semester. After Thanksgiving, her advisor would be in to do a classroom evaluation of her as a teacher.

Where did Jeremy fit into her life? She'd chosen to break up with him, and they might never get together again. Trusting God and waiting for His answers was hard at times.

Jeremy threw himself into preparations for the final ministry team program at Maranatha. At the same time, a plan to reconnect with Aubrey began to form in his mind.

But first things first. Kyle, Renée, and Sarah needed him as an involved team member. He had to trust the Lord to direct him to his heart's desire. The urge to contact Aubrey teased him, but he'd try to respect her wish for distance between them.

Maranatha held a thank-you dinner for the ministry team after the morning worship service. He smiled, shook hands, gave hugs, and said thank you. Though he was grateful for what he'd learned and experienced here as he prepared for future ministry, guilt gnawed at him. He'd allowed himself to be distracted from doing his best today. Nobody said anything, so maybe no one noticed. But he did, and God knew.

As they returned to Clark Seminary, Kyle drove. They talked

about Maranatha for the first part of their trip, then lapsed into silence. Jeremy's thoughts returned to Aubrey.

"What are you doing for Thanksgiving, Jeremy?"

"Huh? Oh. This is reunion year for my mother's family, the Harts. So, the Hart family will all descend on our house in Wellsburg for Thanksgiving."

"I sure hope your family reunion isn't as boring as ours always was." Sarah grumbled from the back seat. "All the old people just sat around and talked about the good old days."

"Wasn't there anyone your age?" Renée asked. "We always have games for the kids while the adults visit. And the food is sooo good that we always stuff ourselves."

"The only ones my age were my brother and sister." Sarah shook her head. "The others were just little kids. The food was okay, and it was all right for a while, but it really got boring after a couple of hours. Mom and Dad wouldn't think of letting us stay home. I haven't been to one since I started college."

Jeremy might be willing to skip the Hart family reunion if he could spend Thanksgiving with Aubrey. But he'd miss it.

"For Thanksgiving, just my immediate family has dinner together." Kyle passed a car. "My whole family gets together at Christmas, and we have fun. We go skating and sledding, have snowball fights. Instead of serious gifts, we each bring a funny gift, one that we buy or make or recycle."

"The Hart family reunion takes place every five years because my relatives are spread across the country and even overseas," Jeremy explained. "I always look forward to the reunions with relatives I seldom see. And Mom looks forward to being together with her family, even though it means a lot of extra work for her. But the family pitches in to help, and we have a great time."

"Will Aubrey be joining you this year?" Sarah leaned forward. She'd hinted more than once that she was available and interested in Jeremy, though he didn't encourage her. Sarah, although an attractive and talented young woman, could never replace Aubrey in Jeremy's heart and mind.

He shook his head. "Not this year. She'll be spending Thanksgiving in Greenlawn with her family."

If it had been just Kyle or just Renée, Jeremy might say more. But he didn't want to confide in Sarah concerning personal issues. She was too nosey.

Kyle looked at him, opened his mouth as though to say more, but closed it without speaking. Relieved, Jeremy watched the passing scenery. He preferred not to discuss Aubrey with the team.

If his plans worked out, however, and he could get away from his family without causing too much bother, he hoped to leave Wellsburg early Sunday morning to be in Greenlawn. He'd attend church with Aubrey and take her out to eat afterward. And, he hoped, convince her of what he already knew: they belonged together.

THE HART FAMILY reunion brought together Jeremy's mother's large family for a boisterous holiday and weekend. The Abbotts' house overflowed with people and food. Jeremy enjoyed getting caught up on Hart family news, seeing his grandparents, and reconnecting with cousins and aunts and uncles, some he hadn't seen for five years.

The shadow of his break-up with Aubrey clung to him. He confided only in Jason.

At daybreak on Sunday, Jeremy left Wellsburg to drive to Greenlawn.

He rang the doorbell at the Whites' house, and Willie opened the door.

"Hey, Willie!" Jeremy looked past him, hoping to see Aubrey. He shivered as a cold gust of wind whipped across his back.

"Hi, Jeremy." Willie frowned and leaned against the door. "Was Aubrey expecting you?"

Why did Willie keep him out in the cold? "No, I wanted to surprise her."

Willie shook his head. "Um, my sister's not here."

"She's not?" Jeremy's heart sank to his toes. "I guess I goofed. I should have called first."

"Who is it, Willie?" Mrs. White came down the stairs in a dress and heels.

"It's Jeremy." Willie turned toward his mother. "Looking for Aubrey."

"Oh, she's not here." Mrs. White came to the door with a smile. "Please, won't you come in, Jeremy? It's cold outside."

Cold outside and inside me, Jeremy thought as he stepped into the house and closed the door.

"I'm surprised you didn't know." She led him into the living room. "Aubrey is at Christina's. She spent Thanksgiving Day here with us and left Friday afternoon to stay for the weekend with Christina. They went to a concert last night. She'll be going directly back to Clark from there."

Jeremy shook his head. "I didn't know." They hadn't talked for over a week. Aubrey must have meant it when she said she wanted to break up. His chest tightened.

"Why don't you stay and have breakfast with us? Then we can go to church together." He could see the questions in Mrs. White's eyes, and he appreciated that she didn't pry.

Misery filled his heart. He couldn't bear to face the White family just then.

Jeremy shook his head. "Thanks for the invitation, but I have some things to do. I'll see you in church, though."

"All right." Mrs. White laid her hand on his arm. "We'll see you in a little while."

"I'll see you out." Willie followed Jeremy out the door and closed it behind them.

They paused on the steps.

"I knew something was going on. My sister didn't talk about you once. I take it you had some sort of falling out?" Willie, without his coat, hunched his shoulders against the cold and slid his hands into his pants pockets.

"You could say that. Aubrey wants to take some time apart to decide if it's God's will for us to continue our relationship."

Willie nodded with a grin. "And you're left hanging because you're sure it is God's will. Don't give up on Aubrey yet, Jer. I think she'll come around."

Maybe he was right. He knew Aubrey well.

A seed of hope implanted itself in Jeremy's heart. "Thanks, friend." He offered his hand, and Willie shook it.

After his long drive this morning, he needed something in his stomach. A cup of coffee and a bagel at the Hillside Diner would help.

AT THE TRACK late on Monday afternoon, Aubrey and Christina had started their run when Jeremy joined them. The sun had just dropped below the western horizon, and the evening star glowed above it.

"Good evening." He greeted them as he fell into step beside Aubrey.

"Hello, Jeremy." Christina gave him a quick smile from Aubrey's other side.

"Hi." Aubrey spoke so softly he barely heard her.

What could he say to ease the tension that stretched the air between them? He had to choose his words carefully and not offend Aubrey or set her off in Christina's presence.

"How was the concert?"

"It was good." Aubrey glanced his way. "Mom said you stopped by the house yesterday."

"Yes, I'm sorry I missed you."

Christina frowned but didn't interrupt them.

The lights along the track came on as a few other students arrived.

At some undistinguished signal, the threesome sprinted the last time around the track, then slowed up, laughing and out of breath. Jeremy had to push hard to stay ahead of the girls. They cooled off with one more slow circuit of the field, then stretched.

"Daniel isn't a runner?" Jeremy asked Christina.

"No, and he dislikes cold air. He's more apt to spend time on the machines in the weight room."

"I'm surprised you're here this afternoon." Aubrey faced him.

"No more ministry team at Maranatha." He couldn't tell by her expression if she was pleased to see him. "I'll have more time to run now. I'll be on campus for the next two weeks, including the weekend."

She didn't comment.

"Well, I'll see you later." He jogged away. Not much progress, but it was a start.

"That was interesting." Aubrey watched Jeremy.

"I think he was trying to transmit a subliminal message to you." Christina faced her.

"What subliminal message?" Aubrey raised her eyebrows.

"Don't count him out. He's still interested."

Aubrey shrugged and began to walk toward the dorm. Running with Jeremy this evening had been unsettling, yet pleasant.

"What did you mean when you said he stopped by the house?" Christina caught up with her.

"He evidently stopped in Greenlawn yesterday for church, expecting to see me." Aubrey pushed some loose strands of hair back from her face. "And I wasn't there."

"Oh, Aubrey."

"It doesn't mean anything." He said he wouldn't give up.

"Don't be cruel. He went all that way just to see you." Christina shook her head. "It means you're crazy not to see the truth. You two belong together."

Aubrey kept walking, unable to deny Christina's words, but she didn't want to admit their truth out loud. She'd completed most of the graduate school application and gathered the information she'd need to apply for the scholarship. She had goals.

Over the next week, the late afternoon runs and seeing Jeremy became an unexpressed high point of her days. The three of them talked about classes and finals, about student teaching and church ministry. With Christina there, Aubrey and Jeremy avoided talking about personal matters that might cause another argument.

On Sunday he appeared at Terrace Baptist in the church aisle beside her. "May I sit with you?" His lips turned up, but his smile didn't reach his eyes.

"I didn't expect to see you here." That sounded rude, and Aubrey wished she could take the words back. She moved over to make space for him.

"I don't have to go to Maranatha with the ministry team, remember?"

She nodded.

"I hope you don't mind my being here."

"No, why should I?" She pretended nonchalance, but her insides fluttered.

"Hey, Jeremy, good to see you." Daniel shook hands with him.

"Hi, Jeremy." Christina looked from him to Aubrey.

Whenever their eyes met, her stomach flip-flopped. Aubrey appreciated that he didn't pressure her with questions, because she had no answers. Yet, she found herself longing for the closeness they'd begun to share during the summer.

As the semester wrapped up, Aubrey had reports and evaluations to submit, not tests, and she met with her advisor to review her teaching experience. She attended workshops and a social gathering for the student teachers and their advisors.

Every day, Jeremy came to the track, ran with them, and talked to them. She remained cool toward him to maintain the boundaries she'd set.

On the last day before vacation, Jeremy met her and Christina at the track.

"Hi, Jeremy." Aubrey wanted to say something that would break the tension but couldn't find the words.

He returned the greeting. They warmed up and began to jog.

"What are your plans for break, Jeremy?" Christina spoke first.

"I'll spend Christmas with my family and then head to Guatemala for ten days."

Aubrey remained silent and kept her eyes on the track ahead. She wanted to know more about his trip but wouldn't ask. If her face didn't already tingle from the cold, it would burn from the memory of her temper tantrum when she first learned about the trip. She should apologize.

"Have you applied to the graduate schools yet, Aubrey?" he asked.

"I just sent in an application." She glanced toward him, not meeting his eyes.

"How about you, Christina?"

"I haven't applied. I may wait a year."

Aubrey expected an engagement announcement from her roommate around Christmas. She watched the track before her. Christina's presence kept her from speaking more personally to Jeremy. So many unsaid words lay between them. Maybe it was better this way. At least it kept them from arguing.

"I'm glad the snow hasn't prevented us from running." She'd never felt so at a loss for something to say. A light coating covered the grass and lay on tree branches. "I think we're supposed to have a white Christmas this year." She expected a comment from Jeremy concerning a "White Christmas." She missed his usual banter.

They cooled down and stretched.

"Have a great vacation." Jeremy nodded to them and left.

Hoping he'd turn back and wave, Aubrey watched his retreating figure for a minute. He didn't. She blamed herself for his drooping shoulders and the lack of spring in his step. She'd set the parameters for their relationship, and he respected them.

She straightened her shoulders and headed for the dorm with Christina.

Tomorrow she'd go home for a well-deserved vacation, with another semester conquered and a step closer to graduation.

Finally, he could go home! The meeting with the Guatemala missions team and their advisor ended the semester for him. His body and mind both needed a few days' rest. The semester had been spiritually and academically rewarding but physically, mentally, and emotionally draining.

What was he to do about Aubrey? He hated the wall between them.

He repeated Psalm 37:4 and 5 to himself, then he prayed. "God, You promised that if I delight in You and commit my way to You, I will have my heart's desires. I don't know why You have allowed this split between us. I love her, and I think in her heart she feels the same about me. But I'm not sure what my next step will be. Please show me what to do."

An inner voice seemed to say, "Wait."

Snow began falling as he left the campus. "Well, Aubrey, I guess you'll get your white Christmas." He turned on the windshield wipers. The snow-covered road forced him to reduce his speed. By the time he arrived home, later than he expected, his body ached from tension.

The winter sun had set, and darkness shrouded the neighborhood when he pulled into the driveway. Human and dog footprints headed down the street side by side. Haleigh must have arrived home earlier.

He got out of the car and stretched, grabbed his luggage, and went inside through the front door.

"I'm home, Mom!" He left his shoes on the throw rug beside the door before walking down the hall to the kitchen.

"Oh, Jeremy, I'm glad you're here. The snow's getting heavy." Mom turned from the kitchen counter to greet him with a hug.

"It's getting slippery. Is Dad home?"

"No, he should be home soon, though. Haleigh took her dog for a walk."

"I saw their footprints in the snow. Did you pick her up from school?"

"No, she found a ride with another student coming this way."

Jeremy went up to his room and turned on the bedside lamp. He set down his luggage and looked around, finding comfort in its familiarity. The bed looked so inviting.

I'll close my eyes for just a few minutes. He lay down, sighed, and relaxed. The next thing he knew, someone was knocking on his open door.

"Wh-what?" He sat up. Where was he?

"Wake up, sleepy head." Haleigh leaned against the doorjamb. "Mom says to tell you supper is ready."

"Oh. Okay. I'll be down in a minute."

She turned and left. He rubbed his eyes and yawned, then ran his hand through his hair. Although glad to be home, he hoped he could avoid another blow-up with Haleigh.

Sunshine met him at the foot of the stairs, her body wiggling furiously.

"Hi, girl." He yawned again as he sat on the bottom step, put his arm around her, and scratched behind her ears, avoiding her tongue. "No, I don't need a kiss from you. But thanks for the thought." In the kitchen, he washed his hands and sat at the table. "Anything I can help you with, Mom?"

"No, we're all set." She placed a bowl of spaghetti sauce on the table while Haleigh poured drinks.

"Hey, Jeremy!" His father entered the kitchen. "Good to see you, Son."

"Hi, Dad." He welcomed his father's embrace. Arms that had always meant love, strength, and comfort.

Once they all had sat down, Dad prayed.

Jeremy and Haleigh answered questions from their parents about school. Several times, Jeremy caught Haleigh looking at him, but she refused to meet his eyes. The air between them like a piece of elastic Haleigh used for sewing, ready to snap if released, they spoke only a few words to each other. He prayed they'd avoid a blow-up.

"Good dinner, Mom." He laid aside his napkin. "The food at school is okay, but it doesn't compare to your good cooking."

"Thank you, Jeremy." She smiled.

"What are your plans, Son?" Dad folded his napkin and placed it next to his plate. "You're leaving for Guatemala on the twenty-seventh, right?"

Haleigh didn't say a word as he laid out his expectations for the trip. Did she miss their old camaraderie as much as he did? Did she feel the empty space left in the family because Jason had left? Did she care enough about the pain in his heart because of his separation from Aubrey to do something about it?

As he and their parents talked, Haleigh got up quietly and began clearing the table, listening but not speaking. His sister had always been laid back, but as they'd grown up, she'd been there to support and encourage him and Jason.

Even when she had pulled back from former friendships, she remained a loyal family member. However, she wouldn't go back to Greenlawn or talk about their friends there.

Jeremy admired her skill with Sunshine and her willingness to help sick and elderly people through the dog therapy program. If he could only discover what from the past held her in its grip, perhaps he could help her renew her friendship with Aubrey.

"Hey, Mom, why don't you go watch the news with Dad?" He pushed back his chair. "Haleigh and I will do the dishes and put the food away."

Haleigh stared at him with raised eyebrows, but she didn't protest.

"I won't argue with that offer." Mom smiled. "Thanks, kids."

After their parents left, Haleigh turned to Jeremy. "So, who's going to wash and who's going to dry?"

"We'll flip a coin." He pulled a quarter out of his pocket. "Heads I wash and you dry."

Haleigh watched as he flipped the coin.

"Heads." He showed her the coin.

She put away leftovers as he ran water into the sink and added dish soap.

After a few minutes, Jeremy broke the silence between them. "You're quiet tonight."

"I didn't have much to add to the conversation." She shrugged. "I guess you're pretty excited about Guatemala."

"I'll be working with my friend Renée's fiancé." He nodded.

"Who's Renée?" She reached for a plate from the dish drainer.

"Renée was a member of my ministry team this semester. Her fiancé is in church planting in Guatemala. The seminary often sends short-term teams there."

"Oh."

"Are you doing anything with Sunshine during Christmas break?" He lifted a mound of dish soap bubbles in his palm and blew them back into the sink.

"Yes, we've been invited to a party for kids in the children's ward at the hospital. Sunshine and I like to go there. The nursing home is having a party for its residents, and Sunshine is always a favorite guest. We'll be helping Santa pass out gifts to any people who have to stay in the hospital over Christmas. You can join us if you'd like."

He felt a nudge against his leg. The black dog looked up at

him with soft brown eyes. "You do have a way about you, Sunshine. When they see your smile, they can't help but smile." He might accept Haleigh's invitation.

"I may be just imagining it, but she seems a little down." Haleigh pulled a plate from the drainer and dried it. "She didn't want to walk as long as usual, and she's spending more time sleeping."

"Maybe it's the weather, the shorter days, and the cold."

"It's never mattered before." Haleigh lifted the stack of plates into the cupboard.

Sunshine sighed as she lay down on the floor near the table.

"I may be going back to Greenlawn for the summer." Haleigh leaned against the counter.

"Really? How come?" Jeremy couldn't hide his surprise at her announcement.

"Remember the Sousas? They built a log cabin home on Woods Road?"

"Yeah, on the outskirts of Greenlawn." Jeremy nodded.

"Well, they called Dad to see if I wanted to house sit. Mr. Sousa has a sabbatical, and the whole family will be gone for a year. They don't want to leave the house empty all that time."

"What do you think?"

"I think it might be time for me to go back." She took a deep breath and twisted the dish towel.

He waited for her to say more, but she began to dry the spaghetti pot. With no dirty dishes remaining, he let the water out of the sink and rinsed the dishcloth.

"Jeremy." Haleigh took a deep breath. "I'm sorry about Aubrey." Her brown eyes met his. "I'm sorry that I've caused trouble between you."

"Thanks, Haleigh." He rested his hand on the counter.

"Are you ... do you ... are you still dating?"

"No, not right now." He saw his face reflected in the window above the sink. "It's complicated. But I haven't given up yet. Willie said he thought she'd come around."

"You've talked to Willie?"

Her wistful tone caught his attention, but she concentrated on putting away the spaghetti pot.

"I saw him after Thanksgiving when I stopped in Greenlawn. Aubrey had gone to a concert with her roommate, Christina, but Willie told me I shouldn't give up."

"He's a good friend."

For over five years, Haleigh had refused to discuss Greenlawn and their friends there. But her friendship with Willie White had withstood the breakup of the Three Sisters. However, as with everything and everyone pertaining to Greenlawn, she'd cast Willie aside after the Abbott family moved away. Now she might return for the summer.

The seed of hope swelled in Jeremy's heart.

"One day I hope you can talk to Aubrey and Katie and Willie, and all your friends in Greenlawn."

"I'll consider it." She hung up the dish towel.

He waited for her eyes to meet his. "No matter what you decide, I'm still going to ask Aubrey to marry me. Not today or tomorrow, but when the time is right. I love her and want to spend the rest of my life with her."

"I'm glad for you." Haleigh pushed a loose strand of long brown hair back from her face. "I want you to be happy."

When he put his arm around her, she leaned her head against him. He hit the light switch as they left the kitchen, a black dog at their heels.

"Hey! Ow!" Aubrey turned from her car to see who had greeted her with the snowball that hit her back.

"Hi, Aubrey. Welcome home." Jesse grinned as he shaped another handful of snow into a ball.

Should've known! She grabbed a handful of snow and charged her brother as she formed a snowball. Splat! Another hit her shoulder. Hers hit him in the chest as her feet slid from under her.

"Ouch!" She lay on her back a minute to catch her breath and assess for injuries.

"Are you okay?" Jesse's concerned face came into view as he bent over her.

Laughing, she grabbed another handful of snow and tossed it in his face. "Gotcha!"

"Hey!" He wiped his face, but his snow-caked glove only made it worse.

"Truce! I need to get my things inside." She stood up and brushed the snow off her clothes.

With a grin, he clapped his hands together to get rid of the snow and grabbed her briefcase and a suitcase from the trunk. Two boxes containing Christmas presents remained.

"What do you have in here, Aubrey?" He grimaced with pretend effort. "Bricks?"

"Mostly clothes in the suitcase, but a few books in the briefcase. Too heavy for ya?" She couldn't resist picking on him. Jesse worked out regularly.

"Ha!"

He held open the door for her, and she preceded him into the house carrying her purse and garment bag.

"How's school?"

"Only one semester to go." Jesse grimaced at her question. Dad had allowed him to get his pilot's license when he agreed to attend the community college for two years. "I'll be glad when May comes." He set down her suitcase and briefcase. "I'll get the rest of your stuff." The door shut behind him.

"Hi, Mom, I'm home!" Aubrey slipped out of her snow-covered shoes and coat and left them by the door.

"I'm in here."

She entered the living room as Mom turned toward her with a smile. The decorated Christmas tree stood in its usual place in front of the window.

"I see Jesse gave you a proper greeting. He still has more energy than the rest of us put together. It's good to have you home."

"The roads are getting slippery, as well as the driveway." She relished Mom's embrace. "I wished for a white Christmas. I guess I have to be careful what I wish for."

Jesse came in stomping his feet. "Here's the rest of your stuff, Aubrey."

"Thanks. I think I'd better get unpacked. I'll be down to set the table, Mom."

Upstairs, she set her suitcase on her bed and hung her garment bag in her closet. She wandered around her lifelong bedroom, decorated in her favorite color, blue. She'd chosen the blue patchwork bedspread, sheer, matching curtains, and the blue-gray carpet while in high school. She paused to look at the framed photo of her with Leanna and the basketball championship trophy on a shelf with other awards.

"This could be my last Christmas at home."

"I know." Jesse came in behind her to set her boxes on the floor. "Me too."

She watched his retreating back. Her little brother had given her a subtle message. What did Jesse have planned? She'd have a big sister talk with him later.

With her things settled, she went back to the kitchen.

"I'm sorry." Willie arrived home from his business in time to eat supper with the rest of the family. "I'll have to eat and run tonight. An order of flowers came in just before closing, so I have to check it in before morning."

"Sounds like you're busy." Aubrey stopped setting the table long enough to give him a hug.

"Swamped. I never thought I'd have this many orders for flowers and centerpieces in Greenlawn. Tia Moreno will be coming in to help now that she's finished her semester finals at the community college. It will quiet down in a few days."

"I'm free now too, if you need my help," Jesse said. "I had my last final this morning."

"Thanks, Jesse. I could use a deliveryman."

"I'll plan to be there in the morning."

"I have to check with Mr. Duncan to see if he needs me at the diner. He said he might. If not, I can help you." Aubrey began to stack plates. "But for tonight, I have a book upstairs that has been begging to be read all semester."

Later, when she returned downstairs with her book, she watched Jesse put on his coat as Willie waited by the door.

"A hot date?" Aubrey asked.

"Not exactly." Jesse shook his head. "Just meeting some friends."

His refusal to meet her eyes made her wonder if a special girl was included among those friends.

"I'm ready, Wills." Jesse pulled on his gloves.

On their way to her father's company's Christmas party, Mom and Dad went out the door at the same time as her brothers. As the quiet settled around her, Aubrey picked up her book to read. After reading two pages three times, she gave up and put the book down.

Had Jeremy made it home safely? What fun it would be to walk through the snow with him.

She put on her coat and boots and stepped out on the back deck. The snow had stopped falling and the back yard lay under a coat of pristine white. Clouds raced across the dark sky, casting shadows as they played hide and seek with the silver moon. Aubrey breathed in the crisp air, remembering last summer when she sat under the tree with Jeremy.

Deciding the yard looked too beautiful to spoil with her footprints, she returned to the kitchen, took off her wet boots, walked to the front door, put the boots back on, and stepped out.

Two sets of tire tracks lined the driveway. She took the snow shovel off the front step and shoveled the driveway and sidewalk.

The physical effort invigorated her. After setting the shovel back in its place, she walked around the block to the house where the Abbotts used to live.

The glow from the streetlights made alternating patches of light and shadow. Christmas lights glowed from lawns and windows, reflecting in a rainbow of colors against the fresh, white snow.

Memories of childhood, friendship, and laughter flickered through her mind. Jeremy had been a part of that. She leaned against the fence at the former Abbott home and gazed at the house outlined with blue Christmas lights.

After Leanna died and sports became less important to her, her career goal to become a teacher had taken precedence in her life. But her focus began to change when an old friendship grew into love.

If she allowed her love for Jeremy to grow, she'd lose control of her plans, of her life. As always, she'd made up her own mind without discussing it with him. She shook her head. She'd shut Jeremy out.

Christina was right. She should have considered Jeremy, not just herself. She loved him, and she may have destroyed any possibility of a future with him.

Wiping tears from her cold cheeks, she turned back toward home. Neighbors shoveling and blowing snow waved or called out greetings. She kicked at a lump of snow the snowplow had thrown up on the sidewalk.

Before reentering the house, she stopped for three deep, cleansing breaths of the crisp air. As she opened the door, the telephone rang. She slid off her boots and ran to answer.

WITH A CUP OF HOT CHOCOLATE, Aubrey returned to the living room and snuggled under an afghan to read her book. Sweetie Pie joined her.

She looked up when Mom and Dad came in the door an hour later.

"Mike called."

"Oh, what did he have to say?" Dad hung his coat in the closet, then turned to take Mom's coat.

"He and Madison will be here in time for the church Christmas Eve service. They'll have to go back Christmas night. Madison's family is having their family get-together on the day after Christmas."

Mom touched an ornament on the Christmas tree. "We'll have all of you home for Christmas this year."

Yes, this could be the last Christmas their family would all be together. Who knew what changes next year might bring for her, for all of them?

After working hard all semester, Aubrey planned to enjoy herself and make this Christmas, perhaps her last one in Greenlawn, special.

Once Mr. Duncan agreed to put her on the schedule to work at Hillside Diner during Christmas break, she called Katie and set up a time to go to the mall and have lunch together.

Wherever she went, Aubrey looked twice at persons whose build, hair, or voice reminded her of Jeremy. Regret nagged her. She picked up her phone several times to text him. Each time she set it down without doing so, uncertain what to say, afraid he wouldn't read her message.

The day after Christmas, Hillside Diner filled with bargain shoppers stopping in for lunch. After-Christmas sales at the mall called to her. Aubrey wished she had time to go.

She finished helping a waitress deliver orders to a table and returned to greet the line of customers waiting to be seated.

"Table for ..." She glanced up into familiar dark brown eyes and a smile.

"Jeremy!" A thrill passed through her, and she smiled back.

"Just one." He held up his index finger.

Breathless and trembling, she nodded, picked up a menu, and

led him to a small table in a corner by the front window. She laid the menu on the table and stood there as he sat.

"Jeremy, I—"

"I'm just passing through." He picked up the menu. "I'm on my way back to the seminary. We leave for Guatemala tomorrow." He smiled up at her.

She pulled her eyes away. A long line of customers waited to be seated. The same problem all over again—no time.

"I have to go." She could hardly squeeze out words. "I don't have time to talk right now."

"I know." He opened the menu. "That's okay. I know you're working."

"A waitress will be with you shortly to take your order."

"Thank you."

Somehow, she managed to smile, welcomed the next customers with poise, and avoided looking toward Jeremy's table every ten seconds. She volunteered to help the busy waitress by taking Jeremy's order to his table a few minutes later. After setting the plate of food on the table, she clasped her hands together, trying to control the tremor.

"Thank you, Goldie."

His smile sent shivers through her. Hearing his special name for her reassured her.

"You're welcome." She remained by his table after checking to see that no customers waited to be seated and watched him put catsup on his burger. "I-I didn't expect to see you here."

"Just a whim." He squirted catsup over his French fries. "I felt like visiting Greenlawn today, and it's not much out of my way."

He could have saved a couple of hours' travel time if he'd gone directly to Clark.

"How was your Christmas?"

"Good." She watched the entrance. No new customers. "It was good." She wanted to say more, but it wasn't the right time and place.

"Look, Aubrey, I know you're busy." He touched her hand, sending electricity through her. "But I had to see you before going away, if only for a minute."

She clasped her hands so she wouldn't grab his and glanced out the window. Several more cars pulled into the parking lot. "I'm glad you did. I've missed you."

A smile lit his face. "Really?"

"I'm sorry for some of the things I said." She spoke softly.

"Aubrey!" A waitress called to her, indicating she needed help carrying an order to another table.

"I have to go."

"I know." He pulled the paper off his straw and inserted it in his glass of cola. "I'll see you when I get back. Oh, and I wanted to tell you that my sister might be living in Greenlawn next summer."

"Really?"

He nodded. His announcement triggered questions in her mind, but she didn't have time for further conversation.

"See you when you get back." She glanced over her shoulder once.

Before picking up his burger, he smiled at her.

The brief encounter left her both exhilarated and dissatisfied. Again, there had been too much left unsaid, too little time for meaningful conversation. She sighed. Now she'd have to wait for two weeks. Patient waiting was not one of her strong points.

THAT NIGHT, she arrived home to find Willie outdoors sweeping a light coating of snow off the sidewalk.

She got out of her car and walked toward the house. "Hi, Wills."

"Hey, Aubrey. How was your day?"

"Busy." She stopped beside him. "How about you?"

"It was almost boring after such a busy season."

They entered the house by the back door into the warm and inviting kitchen.

"Mom, Dad, and Jesse went out for a while." Willie took off his gloves. "Mom said that if you need something to eat, leftovers are in the fridge."

"I had something at the diner. How about some hot chocolate?" She couldn't count the number of times they'd shared hot chocolate after a cold day outdoors in winter.

"Sounds good." He rubbed his hands together.

After hanging up their coats, they left their shoes by the back door.

"Marshmallows?" He took two mugs out of the cupboard as she heated a pan of milk on the stove and added chocolate syrup. At her nod, he dropped three large ones into each mug.

She poured the fragrant liquid into the mugs, and they sat down at the kitchen table across from each other.

"Now that Christmas is over, how do you feel your first season in business has been?" She wrapped her cold hands around the warm mug.

"Unbelievable. God has blessed me so much." He blew on the hot chocolate. "Greenlawn is a good town for a florist business. I'm surprised no one started one here before now." He tested a sip. "I'm going to expand into landscaping in the spring. Jesse said he'd work with me."

"Are you planning to set up a website?"

"I'll do that in January, during the slow season. The florist business will pick up around Valentine's Day, then slack off until spring."

"Sounds like a good plan." She pushed her marshmallows down into her hot chocolate with her spoon. "I had a visitor at the diner this afternoon."

"Oh?"

She licked her spoon. "Jeremy."

"I suppose he had a reason."

"He's leaving for Guatemala tomorrow." She shrugged. "He stopped off in Greenlawn on his way to the seminary." Avoiding her brother's eyes, she traced the lip of her mug with her index finger. Jeremy had come to see her despite all she'd said to discourage him.

"And he wanted to see a certain somebody, I imagine." Willie's eyes crinkled with a smile. "I didn't think you really wanted to let him go."

The heat in her face wasn't from the hot chocolate. She didn't deny his statement. "But he told me something you'll be interested in knowing." She pushed her marshmallows into the hot drink with her fingertip, then licked her finger.

He set down his mug and raised his eyebrows. "Oh?"

"He said Haleigh might be coming to Greenlawn for the summer." She watched him for his response.

"H-Haleigh?" He stared at her. "Coming back to Greenlawn?"

"I know." She leaned her elbows on the table. "It surprised me too."

"Did he say why?" He looked down as he spun his mug on the table.

"No, we didn't have much time to talk. But I knew you'd want to know."

"Yeah." Her brother stirred his drink, picked up the almost melted marshmallows with his spoon, and dropped them back into the mug. He probably didn't realize what he was doing.

"Willie." She waited until he looked up at her. "If you cared that much, why didn't you go after her?"

He swallowed and pushed his fingers through his hair, a gesture that reminded her of Jeremy. Resting his arms on the table, he leaned forward. "At first I didn't know how to help her. We were both young, and she hurt so much. Once the Abbotts moved, she refused to answer letters, emails, or phone calls. You know that."

"I know."

"She never returned with her family to visit. I decided she

didn't want my friendship, so I went on with my life, hoping she'd one day change her mind."

"And now?"

"Now, I don't know." He sat back. "Maybe there's a reason she's coming back now. Maybe God has something in mind."

"For the two of you?"

"Maybe." He shrugged. "If she does come back, I'll find out. And if she doesn't come here next summer, I may pay her a visit. I feel like we have some unfinished business."

"How did you do it, Wills?" She laid her hand on his wrist. "I mean, you've waited a long time. If you're not careful, you'll become Greenlawn's most eligible young bachelor, and you'll have all the young women buying your flowers just for the opportunity to catch your eye."

Aubrey knew of several girls in their hometown who'd jump at the chance to date Willie. Unlike Jesse, who basked in female attention, Willie had an inoffensive way of remaining friendly without encouraging romantic notions.

The corners of his mouth turned up, and she snickered.

"I worked on my other goals while deciding what to do about Haleigh." He took a final drink of hot chocolate. "I know she's not the only girl out there. It's just that I can't get her out of my mind. We have to be sure our direction comes from God. Isn't that what Mom and Dad have always taught us?"

Maybe last semester hadn't been God's time for her and Jeremy. Aubrey picked up their empty mugs, rinsed them, and placed them in the dishwasher. She inhaled deeply and exhaled before she turned back toward her brother.

"Maybe God will give both of us a second chance." He grinned.

She held up her hand with her fingers folded into her palm. His knuckles bumped hers.

AUBREY'S PHONE RANG. Christina.

"Guess what, Roomie?"

That wasn't hard to figure. "Daniel asked you to marry him, you said yes, and now you're wearing a diamond ring."

"Yes, yes, and yes. How did you guess?" She giggled.

"I'm glad for you, Christina." Aubrey took a deep breath. "Congratulations." She tamped down the twinge of envy that grabbed at her. Leaving the book she'd been reading open, she got up from the chair at her desk and pulled aside the window curtain. Snowing again.

"Thank you, Aubrey. It happened yesterday. He came for dinner, and afterward we took a walk in the snow. He proposed in front of the Christmas tree in the town square. It was so romantic!"

What could she say that would be as exciting? Should she tell Christina about Jeremy's appearance? "I got my white Christmas. It's snowed a little each day for the last week. Mike and Madison came Christmas Eve, so all of us were here for Christmas Day."

"Have you heard from Jeremy?"

"He stopped in the diner for lunch today." She sat on her bed. "He was on his way to the seminary. They leave for Guatemala tomorrow."

"And ...?"

Aubrey shrugged then remembered her friend couldn't see her. "The diner was busy, so I didn't have time to talk with him more than a minute or two." She twisted a lock of her hair. "I think I made a mistake, Christina. I couldn't have my way, so I broke off with him instead of trying to work things out. Not that we had an official understanding or anything."

"Don't kid yourself, Aubrey." Christina spoke sternly. "The chemistry between you two was obvious to everybody. Actually, it's more than that." She continued before Aubrey could protest. "I think God intends you for each other. I don't think Jeremy will give up easily."

"Did you and Daniel set a date?" Aubrey wanted time to

process Christina's words and her own thoughts before she talked more about her relationship with Jeremy. And she had to talk to Jeremy himself. "You're still planning to wait a while?"

"We decided not to wait. I'm not sure I want a long engagement We don't have a date, but it will probably be late summer or early fall. We'll see."

"Well, we'll have to start looking at bridal websites when the new semester begins. It'll be fun." Aubrey wanted to mean her words. She wanted to help her friend plan the perfect wedding.

On Monday, Aubrey met a prospective student whose parents had immigrated from India, one with Native American background, one from New York City, and one from a nearby town. She loved showing off the beautiful Clark campus to visitors and sharing personal experiences about her time at Clark.

Remembering her first visit to the campus, she tried to assure the nervous, prospective students that Clark would be their best choice. In between tours, she worked in the admissions office, sorting correspondence and mailing out catalogs and financial aid information.

In late afternoon, after work, she ran on the track. The short days and the cold, snowy weather since her return to campus a week before spring semester began made it less appealing to get dressed and go out. She ate in the college commons with the few students who'd already returned to campus.

The evening would be long and lonely without her roommate, but she'd have time to think about Jeremy and pray about their relationship.

She opened her computer. Neither a message from the graduate school nor one from Jeremy appeared on the screen.

On Tuesday, Jeremy sent her an email with a photo of a village.

Dear Goldie,

The weather here is warm, the coffee is great, and the people are so hospitable. The poverty breaks my heart. I feel so selfish and so blessed. The scenery is breathtaking. I wish you could see all this with me. Internet access is not available much of the time, so I can't write often. I'll tell you all about it when I get back. I miss you.

As always,
Jeremy

Uncertain whether he'd receive it, Aubrey sent him a return email.

The day before she expected him to be back at the seminary, she received a postcard from him with a breathtaking view of mountains.

JEREMY SIGHED as he slipped his laptop under the seat ahead of him, buckled his seat belt, and leaned back in his seat on the plane. He regretted the shortness of his time in Guatemala.

The missions team from Clark Seminary worked side-by-side with Guatemalan Christians as they constructed a new church building and held outdoor evangelistic services. Jeremy loved the people and appreciated their hospitality. He'd taken a lot of photos.

A few times, he and his teammates had to trust God when they met hostility toward the 'rich' Americans and their Christian message.

Renée's fiancé, Tyson, the project coordinator, talked to Jeremy about his upcoming wedding and how his ministry would change with a wife beside him. In his luggage, Jeremy carried a letter from Tyson to Renée.

As the plane took off from the airport for the trip home, he anticipated his return to Clark Seminary and his next semester there. He had so much to learn to be ready for full-time ministry, whether in the United States or a foreign country.

To be honest, he'd enjoy sleeping in a real bed rather than on the cot he'd used for more than a week.

Home also meant seeing Aubrey. He'd sent her only one email and a postcard while away, even though he thought of her often. He wanted to give her the space she requested. Her response to his appearance in Greenlawn the day after Christmas and her reply email message to him while he was in Guatemala gave him hope for a complete reconciliation.

For the first hour on the plane, Jeremy and his seatmate talked with the team members in the seat across the aisle about their experiences. As they settled in for the remainder of the flight, Jeremy succumbed to the fatigue that spread over his body, and he slept. He awoke with a scratchy throat and a heaviness in his head.

A cold? Really? Why now?

The pilot's voice over the plane's intercom told them they'd land soon, and she thanked them for flying with the airline. When the *fasten seatbelt* light flashed on, he did so. In another couple of hours, he'd be back at Clark and Aubrey.

THE SUN and crisp air welcomed the first day of the semester as students returned to Clark for registration. Cleared sidewalks crisscrossed the snow-covered campus.

Aubrey and Christina met Daniel and a group of friends in the Commons for lunch. They talked about vacation, compared class schedules, and discussed the semester ahead.

As she listened to the conversations around her, Aubrey

experienced both nostalgia and anticipation. Her last semester at Clark! Soon another milestone would be passed, and the future stretched ahead, uncertain yet exciting. She expected to hear from a graduate school before May.

The urgency to be accepted for the summer dimmed at the thought of being with Jeremy again. Fall would be soon enough to begin the next phase of her goals.

"I have a few things to pick up at the bookstore." Aubrey checked her coat pocket for her wallet. "I'm also going to check out the condition of the track."

Daniel chuckled. "You're a dedicated runner."

"You and Christina are welcome to join me. I thought I'd take a run before dark."

"No, thanks." He shook his head. "We're hanging out together for the rest of the day."

"I'll pass on running for today." Christina put on her coat. "But we'll have to start a regular schedule again, weather permitting."

"Maybe we should sign up for the workout room because we know the weather can get pretty bad around here in the winter." Aubrey preferred to run, but the snow and cold made that impossible at times.

"You may be right." Christina and Daniel followed Aubrey outside and headed for the student center.

Enjoying the day, Aubrey strolled along, grateful for her winter jacket. She called greetings to several friends. In the distance, among the many students crossing the campus, she spotted a familiar figure coming her way. She squinted. A current of excitement passed through her.

She waved, and he waved back when he saw her. She hurried her step, keeping herself to a fast walk.

"Jeremy," she whispered.

He raised his arm and coughed into his elbow. His step didn't have its usual spring, and when she got closer, she could see dark circles under his eyes.

"Are you all right?" Of course, he wasn't. She couldn't think how else to open the conversation.

"Hey, Goldie." His voice was hoarse. He shook his head. "I just went to the clinic. The doctor thinks it's a cold, and they gave me some cough medicine and decongestant." He coughed again, then smiled. "But it's good to see you again."

Aubrey felt herself blushing under his gaze, so much like pools of chocolate. She'd tried to shut him out of her life and didn't deserve his willing acceptance. "I guess you had a good trip."

"It was great! This isn't a great way to return to campus though. A few others who were with me in Guatemala were in the clinic. What are you up to?"

"I'm headed to the bookstore for supplies, then I'm going for a run. Want to come?"

"I'd go with you, but the doctor said I should go to bed. And the way I feel, I think it's a good idea. But I'll walk with you to the bookstore. It's not that much out of my way." He coughed again. "I'd hoped to have time to spend with you this afternoon. I'm sorry."

"Please take care of yourself and get better. Then we'll talk." She added, "I missed you."

His smile melted her heart. "If I take a nap and feel better later, will you have supper with me at the café tonight?" He coughed again and took out a tissue to blow his nose.

"I'd like that, but please don't push yourself too much. Why don't you give me a call when you wake up, and we'll make our plans then."

"N—" He paused and nodded. "Probably that would be best. I don't want to give everybody else my germs."

"If I don't hear from you by five, I'll go to the Commons instead. That way you won't be obligated to come out if you don't feel up to it."

They parted in front of the bookstore. He walked away, his

shoulders hunched in his winter jacket. He coughed several times, then turned and waved once.

Remembering her mission, she entered the bookstore and made her purchases. She didn't have to work in the admissions office today, because no visits or interviews were scheduled on days when students registered for classes.

She returned to the dorm, changed, and did her laps around the track. Back in her room, she checked her schedule and made sure she had everything ready for the next day. She showered and dressed, then lay back on her bed, waiting for Jeremy's call.

The musical tones of her phone startled her awake. Jeremy.

As soon as she answered and heard his cough, she knew they'd have to put off their date for another time.

"Oh, Jeremy, you sound awful!"

"I know," he croaked. "I'll have to give you a rain check for tonight's supper. Why do I have to be sick now?"

"Go take a hot shower, take your medicine, and go to bed." She wrinkled her nose at the motherly tone of her voice. "But will you text me in the morning to let me know how you are?"

"Hey, are you trying to boss me?" He sneezed. "I'll be fine." He sneezed again. "But thank you for caring. I'll let you know."

"Goodnight, Jer."

"Goodnight, Goldie."

After heating a bowl of chicken noodle soup in the dorm lounge microwave, Jeremy rolled into bed early and slept fitfully for the first half of the night, dreaming he was back in Guatemala, looking for Aubrey who was lost in the jungle. Then he fell into a restful sleep.

He awoke in the morning with Aubrey on his mind, along with a mental to-do list for the day. Today he had to wash clothes and get his books for classes. Later he'd meet with his advisor. He showered and shaved, then picked up his phone and speed-dialed Aubrey's number.

"How are you this morning?" she asked.

Talking and laughing sounded in the background. How unfair that others could be with her without him! Of course, she was probably in the Commons having breakfast.

A sudden burst of loud male laughter over her phone made him frown.

"Who's that?" He sounded more abrupt than he intended.

"It's just Mac. He's eating with us this morning."

Mac. Who was Mac? Had he met him? He fought a surge of jealousy since he still feared losing Aubrey.

"Mac is an education major," she explained. "We've had a lot of classes together, and we both did our student teaching last semester."

The friend with red hair. He'd never met Mac, but she'd pointed him out once on campus.

"You didn't answer my question." Impatience edged her voice.

This wasn't how he'd planned his conversation with her. "Oh, sorry. I'm feeling a lot better."

"That's good."

"I've got to get my schedule worked out today. Meet with my advisor, sign up for ministry, and confirm classes. But I want to see you later. Maybe we can eat at the café tonight?"

"I'd like that," she said. "I have to work this afternoon for a couple of hours. Since I'll be on campus this semester, I'm working in the admissions office, giving campus tours to prospective students. Will you meet me in front of the admissions office at five?"

"I'll plan on it. I promise not to keep you out late."

AFTER HER AFTERNOON World Cultures class, Aubrey took her books to her room. She brushed her hair back and fastened it with a barrette, then hurried to arrive in time for work.

As she entered the admissions office, the receptionist smiled at her. She rolled her chair away from her computer and stood to lift a file from a corner table.

"Good afternoon, Aubrey. How were your classes today?"

"I had a good day, Denise. I'm looking forward to the semester." Aubrey took the file and opened it, glancing at the information.

"This is your last semester, right? Are you going to teach next year, or go to graduate school?"

"Well, I plan to teach, but I've also applied to grad school. I'd like to get a master's degree in special education." She could follow that part of Plan A and still have time for Jeremy, right?

Denise came around her desk, and Aubrey turned toward the reception area.

"Aubrey, this is Tucker Leon and his mother, Patricia Leon. Tucker, Patricia, Aubrey White is your campus guide today."

A man and woman stood and stepped forward. Aubrey's first impression was of a small, well-dressed blond woman, and a tall, muscular young man.

"Welcome to Clark University," Aubrey said, shaking hands with the woman first.

The firmness of the man's grasp made her look up into intense blue eyes and a smile that drew her in. She let go of his hand, broke eye contact, stepped back, and took a deep breath. This was no eighteen-year-old high school senior. The young man before her had the mature build of a warrior. Probably a soldier.

"Miss White." He spoke with a deep, quiet voice.

"Please, call me Aubrey. Welcome to Clark University." She turned toward the door. "We'll go this way first." She focused on the mother, trying to quell her inner turmoil. She knew the attraction to Tucker was purely physical, but it had startled her, especially because she'd been thinking about Jeremy all day.

Please help me, Father God. I don't want to make a fool of myself or dishonor You. I know almost nothing about Tucker. Control my thoughts and my reaction to him.

The sidewalks were clear of the ice and snow that covered the lawns. Aubrey explained the layout of the campus and talked about the professors and classes. Tucker remained attentive to his mother even as he asked questions and listened to Aubrey. She felt his eyes on her several times.

"This is the campus bookstore." She gestured toward the building as they approached the glass doors of the building. "I love going in here. It's a beautiful store, and it would be easy to browse for hours."

Tucker held the door open and followed Aubrey and his mother in. Jeremy stood by the cash register paying for his purchases. With Jeremy standing there, she had to remind herself that she was working.

When he saw her, his face lit up. A question entered his dark eyes when he saw her companions.

Her own reaction to Tucker made her think she knew Jeremy's thoughts.

"Hi, Jeremy." She smiled at him and led Tucker and his mother over to a display near the cash register.

"Hi, Aubrey. I guess you're working?"

They attracted the attention of the Leons. She saw Tucker taking Jeremy's measure.

"Patricia, Tucker, I'd like you to meet Jeremy Abbott. He's a first-year seminary student. Jeremy, Tucker is thinking about becoming a student at Clark University next year."

"It's nice to meet you." Jeremy shook hands with Patricia, then Tucker. "Have you enjoyed your tour?"

"Aubrey has been quite thorough." Tucker nodded. "This is a beautiful campus. It's restful, especially compared to some of the places I've been."

"Military?"

"Army. I decided to serve my country before attending college. Now Uncle Sam will help pay for my education."

"It's a relief for this mother that he's not going back." Mrs. Leon laid her hand on her son's arm. "I could hardly stand to watch the evening news while he was overseas."

"I understand." Aubrey nodded. "My youngest brother wants to join the Air Force."

Jeremy's eyes widened. He started to speak but bit his lip instead. She'd tell him more later.

"I'm glad I served, but now it's time to move on to the next phase of my life." Tucker shared a look with his mother, and she nodded.

"Take a few minutes to look around, if you'd like to." Aubrey checked her watch. "I have a few more places to show you, so we'll have to leave soon."

"See you later, Aubrey." Jeremy moved toward the door.

"Okay." She watched him go out the door, then switched her focus back to Tucker and his mother as they browsed through the book section.

A few minutes later, Tucker held the door while his mother and Aubrey exited the store.

Outside, Tucker turned to Aubrey. "Mom and I will be stopping to eat before we go home. Will you join us?"

Aubrey looked from Tucker to his mother, who smiled at her. She hadn't expected an invitation to dinner. However, most of the prospective students to whom she showed the campus still attended high school.

"Thank you. It's kind of you, but I have plans for tonight." She led them toward the next stop on their tour, the sports and fitness center. Tucker would appreciate the up-to-date facility.

"Have you known Jeremy long?"

His question surprised her. Their encounter with Jeremy had been brief, and she had simply introduced them to each other. "Jeremy and I grew up together."

"He's a lucky guy. I hope he knows that." He pulled open the center's heavy, glass door.

"Thanks, Tucker." He had no idea what she and Jeremy had been going through lately.

"I can tell by the way you treat your mother that the girl you marry will be blessed." She followed Patricia inside. He'd treated his mom with gentle courtesy throughout the tour.

"Tucker let me tag along today." Patricia gave her hand a quick squeeze. "I try not to be a clingy mother, but since he'd been away so long, he indulged me. I'm blessed to be his mom." Patricia's eyes held her son's for a brief moment.

They finished the tour back at the admissions office. Aubrey handed Tucker the usual packet of information she gave prospective students. "Do you have any more questions?"

"You've covered the information I needed. Clark is at the top of my school choices." He held out his hand. "Thank you, Aubrey."

Aubrey shook his hand, and Patricia gave her a hug. They said goodbye and Tucker glanced at her once more before shutting the door behind them.

OUTSIDE THE ADMISSIONS OFFICE, Jeremy paced as he waited for Aubrey. He didn't own Aubrey. They had no official commitment to each other. But the thought of losing her to another man didn't sit well with him.

When she and Tucker entered the bookstore earlier, they made a striking couple. He'd noticed the way Tucker looked at her. He raised his hand to wave at the Leons when they left the building, then inhaled and exhaled with relief when Aubrey appeared.

For the next hour or so, he, Jeremy Abbott, would have her company and her attention.

One day soon he'd ask her to marry him. Gram's sapphire ring waited snugly in the corner of his top dresser drawer.

Aubrey had loved Gram. He thought she'd like the ring. If not, he'd get her a different engagement ring.

In a relatively quiet corner of the seminary café, they found a table. After they said grace and began to eat, Jeremy paused before putting a forkful of food in his mouth. "What's this about Jesse going into the Air Force?"

She swallowed a bite of food. "He'll graduate from the community college in May and has decided to join the Air Force. He has a pilot's license and loves to fly. He's been considering it for a long time."

"When will he go?"

"I think he's looking into a program that will allow him to join in the fall." She rested her wrist against the table with her fork in her hand. "Mom's a little worried that he'll be sent to a war zone. I guess I am too. But he needs a way to channel his endless energy, and the military may be just the place for him."

As he took a bite of chicken, Jeremy thought a moment about the news. Then he decided to plunge into what was really on his mind.

"So, do you think Tucker will come to Clark next year?"

"It's hard to tell." She responded with a shrug. "He seemed interested."

"Maybe his interest was in a certain attractive blue-eyed, blond campus guide." He didn't want to start an argument. Because of their recent history, he had to know.

Aubrey's eyes widened. "What do you mean?" She set down her fork.

"I apologize if I'm out of line." Jeremy looked at his plate and then at her again. "I saw the way he looked at you, and I was afraid you ...." He couldn't complete his sentence.

"I'm sorry, Jeremy." Her cheeks turned pink, and she picked up her fork. "I hope nothing in the way I acted toward Tucker made you think I had an interest in him on a personal level." She sighed. "He's an attractive man, and I believe he's looking for God's direction for his future, but I don't think he'll come here just because of me." She moved the food on her plate with her fork. "He said ... he said you're a lucky guy."

His eyebrows rose and his mouth fell open. "He said that?"

She nodded.

"To be honest, Aubrey, since September I've felt as though I've been walking on eggshells as far as our relationship is concerned. I don't feel like a lucky guy. When I saw you with Tucker, I was afraid I might lose you."

"I'm sorry, it hasn't been a spectacular few months for me either." She pushed her food around some more and set her fork down, then looked up. "Can we try again?"

Her expression held an appeal and her blue eyes drew him in.

"Is that what you want, Aubrey?" He leaned across the small

table toward her as his eyes traveled from her eyes to her lips and back again. He wanted to hold her, feel the softness of her hair, assure her of his devotion.

As she drew in a breath, he waited for her answer, his heart picking up speed. For a moment he forgot their public setting. Only the two of them.

"Yes."

"Me too." He smiled.

"Hi, Jeremy. Is this Aubrey?"

Startled, he leaned back and looked up at the dark-haired woman standing beside their table. "Oh, hi, Sarah." He stood politely, watching Aubrey's reaction.

Aubrey sighed and followed him with her eyes as he stood.

"I'm Sarah." She smiled and held out her hand to Aubrey. "Jeremy and I were on ministry team together last semester."

"It's nice to meet you." Aubrey shook Sarah's hand. "Jeremy spoke often about the ministry team."

"Did you get your assignment for this semester yet?" Sarah quickly fixed her eyes on Jeremy and turned with her back toward Aubrey. "Maybe we'll be assigned together again."

"I requested a local assignment this semester." Jeremy glanced helplessly at his dinner mate. "An opening became available as an intern in a church just ten miles from here. I learned a lot at Maranatha, but the time commitment because of the distance is too much for this semester." He glanced again at Aubrey.

"Oh." Sarah's face fell. "Well, I have to go. Have fun, kiddos." She started to move away and then stopped. Leaning down toward Aubrey, she spoke in a conspiratorial tone. "Do you know how lucky you are?" She glanced at Jeremy, then walked away.

Jeremy sat, his shoulders slumped.

"What do you think Sarah meant by that?" Aubrey smiled as she picked up her fork, with a Grandpa White twinkle in her eyes.

"I'm irresistible?" He tipped his head and batted his eyelashes.

Aubrey laughed aloud, then looked around to see if she'd attracted any attention from other diners. She cleared her throat and started eating again.

Jeremy quietly finished his meal and waited for Aubrey to finish. "I don't believe in luck, Goldie. I think God wants us to be together." His eyes locked with hers.

"Me too," she whispered and laid down her fork.

Seeing that she'd finished eating, he cleared his throat again. "We both have studying to do, so we'd better go." Jeremy stood and waited for Aubrey to do the same. "I told you I wouldn't keep you out late, and this cold is making me more tired than usual."

They placed their dishes on the conveyor belt to the kitchen. He helped her with her coat and put on his. If only his time with Aubrey didn't have to end for tonight, but she had studying to do, and he had to prepare for tomorrow. He sauntered by her side toward her dorm.

Lights reflected off the snow-covered ground. Laughter came from across the campus. The notes of a trumpet sounded out. Couples and small groups of students strolled along the sidewalks.

"I've decided not to join the track team this semester," Aubrey said. "I like being on the team, but it takes a lot of time."

"Are you sure?" He didn't want her to have regrets.

"I'm sure. I'll still be able to work with the challenged athletes when the team goes. The coach will post the schedule for that soon. I just won't be training or competing with the team."

He appreciated what she'd sacrifice. "Thank you. It will give us more time to be together." He didn't want a repeat of last semester's frustrations.

"Maybe we can start studying together in the library."

"Is that what you want?" He hunched his shoulders against

the cold air. "It might be too distracting." But no more distracting than not being able to see her last semester.

"Do you think so?" She pushed her hands into her coat pockets.

"We won't be able to have discussions there." He smiled. "But at least we'll be together more."

"I'd like that." Maybe the time they'd spent apart had reaped some benefits. She wanted to be with him now.

"If we can't make it some nights, we'll let each other know. Shall we plan on tomorrow night?"

"Yes, Jeremy, that will be perfect."

19

Saturday morning, Aubrey pulled her hair into a ponytail and took a jacket from the closet. Dressed for running, she opened the door just as her phone went off. Checking to see if it disturbed the still-sleeping Christina, Aubrey closed the door and answered, trying to keep her voice soft.

"Hello ... Yes this is she ... Yes, he was one of my students ... Oh, no!" Her knees shaking, she sat on the edge of her bed. "Of course ... Northeast Medical Center." Aubrey walked to her desk and wrote on a paper. She took a huge breath. "Thank you for calling. Greg is special to me ... Yes, I'll be sure to let you know how he is. 'Bye.'"

Aubrey shut down her phone and leaned her hands on the desk.

"Is everything okay?" Christina sat up in her bed, her eyes puffy with sleep and her voice crackly.

Tears welled in Aubrey's eyes as she turned toward her roommate. "I'm sorry, I didn't mean to wake you up."

"Bad news?" Christina yawned.

"Remember I told you about Greg Adams, the special needs student in my fourth-grade class?" Aubrey sat on her bed.

183

Christina nodded.

"That was the dean of women." Aubrey held up her phone. "Greg's father called her. Greg was in an auto accident with his mother and sister. They're okay, only minor injuries, but Greg's shunt that drains the fluid from his head has malfunctioned." She wiped her eyes with a tissue.

"Is there anything they can do?" Christina got up and came over to Aubrey and put her arms around her.

"The neurosurgeon is going to replace the shunt." Aubrey sniffed and nodded. "The surgery is scheduled for eleven o'clock."

"Do you want me to go with you?"

She heard her roommate's offer, but she had something else on her mind. "Oh, Christina, Greg asked for me. He wants me to come and pray for him."

"Wow!"

"I never talked directly to any of the students about my faith." Aubrey went to her closet to find clothes to wear to the hospital. "I'm not sure why Greg has asked me to pray. I'd pray for him anyway, and I want to see him."

"Let me call Daniel and get dressed." Christina hurried to the closet. "I'll go with you. I don't want you driving alone when you're upset."

Aubrey stood still, then turned to face her friend. "Christina, I know you have plans with Daniel today, and you have a paper to write this weekend." She laid her hand on her roommate's arm. "Don't take this the wrong way, but I think I'll ask Jeremy to go with me instead."

"No offense taken." Christina grinned. "But if Jeremy can't go, I'll be available."

By now he was probably at the track and thought she'd stood him up. Aubrey checked the time as she speed-dialed Jeremy.

He answered immediately. "I was just about to call you. I thought you'd either overslept or decided not to come."

"No, I'm up, but I have to change our plans for today."

"What's wrong?"

"One of my former students is in the hospital. I-I have to go see him."

"Where?"

"Northeast Medical Center."

"Let me change and get my car. I'll be over in about fifteen minutes to pick you up."

"Jeremy, I ... you ..." She stopped to take a breath and collect her thoughts. "You will?"

"Of course, Goldie. Fifteen minutes." He clicked off.

"I never asked him." She stared at her phone, then looked at her roommate. "He just said he'd come. It's like he read my mind over the phone."

"You crazy girl. He loves you. Go, get ready!" Christina gave her a little shove.

Propelled into action, Aubrey stood ready at the dormitory door when Jeremy pulled into the parking lot.

She punched the hospital name into her phone's GPS, and they were on their way. A fresh covering of snow lay on the ground and trees, but the roads were clear. Aubrey shivered from anxiety and cold.

"Cold?" Jeremy glanced at her.

"A little."

"We'll be toasty warm in a few minutes. There's a blanket in the back seat if you want it."

"I'll be okay once the car warms up." She shivered again and hunched her shoulders, holding her gloved hands in front of the vent.

As she warmed up, she studied his profile. "How did you know?"

"Know what, Goldie?" He reduced his speed to accommodate a slower-moving mini-van ahead of them.

"How did you know I was going to ask you to go to the hospital with me?"

"I didn't really know. I just knew you were upset. Your

voice shook, and it takes a lot to get you worked up like that. And I knew you shouldn't be driving by yourself, so I volunteered."

"But what about your schoolwork?"

"Don't worry. I have my trusty laptop with me." He pointed over his shoulder with his thumb toward the back seat.

"Thanks, Jeremy." She nodded and looked out the windshield at the road ahead.

He laid his hand on top of hers. Even through her glove and his, her hand tingled. She looked at their hands, then up at his face.

"This is something we can do together." He smiled.

No longer shivering from the cold, her awareness of his proximity sent a tremor throughout her body.

"Tell me about this student of yours. What makes it so urgent for you to go to the hospital to see him?"

"I never told him I was a Christian." She removed her hand from under his, took a breath, and pulled her ponytail over her shoulder. "But he asked me to come and pray for him before he has his shunt replaced."

"That's great," Jeremy said softly.

"Greg loves to learn. He always wanted to help, and his smile always made my day. I never heard him say or do anything to hurt anyone. He forgave a girl who bullied him, and they became good friends. He's one reason I decided to get my master's degree in special education."

"Do you have another reason?" He passed the van ahead of them.

She slanted her knees toward him so she could look more directly at him. She'd never shared this with anyone, not even Willie or Christina.

"I want whatever I do to really count for something. The challenged kids my track team works with made me realize how much they can accomplish with help and encouragement. I want kids like Greg to have the opportunity to reach their full potential. I want them to know God loves them and has created them for a purpose."

Did he understand how important this was to her?

"You're a beautiful, compassionate, capable woman, Aubrey. I know God has special plans for you." He turned in at the hospital visitors' lot. "I only hope those plans will include me."

Would he believe her assurances that she wanted him to be a big part of her future after she'd denied him so adamantly?

"Any news about graduate school or a scholarship?" He parked the car.

"Not yet. There's still plenty of time."

He opened the car door for her, and they walked together through the sliding glass doors into the hospital. Aubrey reached for Jeremy's hand and held on as they got visitors' passes at the information desk and instructions on where to find Greg's family in the pediatric ICU waiting room.

A man with thinning brown hair and wire-rimmed glasses stood as they entered the waiting room. "Miss White, thank you for coming."

"Mr. Adams, please call me Aubrey." She shook his hand. "How is Greg?"

"They're getting him ready now. He's been asking for you. You remember my wife and daughter, Maureen and Colleen? And I'm Shawn."

Maureen had bruises on her face, and her hand was wrapped in a bandage.

Aubrey introduced Jeremy.

"You're Greg's teacher." Colleen, probably four or five, leaned forward on the couch where she sat beside her mother. "We saw you at Greg's play."

Aubrey knelt and looked directly into her face. "Well, I was his student teacher for a while."

"We had a accident. We crashed. Mommy was driving."

"So I heard, Colleen. I'm glad you're okay."

"Greg didn't get hurt much either, except the impact may

have jarred his shunt." Greg's mother spoke in a trembling voice. "I-I feel responsible. I hurt my son." Tears filled her eyes.

"You didn't mean to, Mommy." Colleen patted her mother's arm. "It was a accident."

The woman hugged her daughter. "I know, sweetie."

"Sometimes shunts have to be replaced. This may have happened without the accident." Shawn squeezed his wife's shoulder, and she smiled up at him.

"Mr. and Mrs. Adams—Shawn and Maureen—Aubrey and I believe in the power of prayer," Jeremy said. "Will you let us pray with you and for Greg?"

"Greg begged for us to ask Miss White to come." Shawn removed his glasses and rubbed his eyes. "He said she'd pray for him. I guess we all need it right now."

They made a circle and joined hands. Jeremy prayed. Overcome with the sense of God's presence, Aubrey closed her eyes, and tears slid down her cheeks.

She knew she wanted this man of faith with her for the rest of her life.

Although she wasn't a family member, the surgeon gave permission for Aubrey to see Greg because the boy had requested her visit. She donned gloves, a mask, and a gown before entering. The unit was partitioned by curtains and windows. Nurses and other staff moved quietly and efficiently about, caring for their young patients. Greg's nurse smiled at her as she finished checking Greg and moved away.

When she caught sight of the boy lying in bed attached to tubes and machines, Aubrey hesitated. Her stomach clenched. She'd awakened in the hospital after her accident to the sound of beeps and hisses. How much more frightening for nine-year-old Greg than for her as a teen.

"Hello, Greg." She approached his bed, hoping he'd recognize her behind the mask.

His eyes opened, and when he focused on her, he smiled. "Hi, Miss White."

She held his free hand in both her own. When she finished praying, she could see his body relax. The smile remained as his eyes closed. "I'll be out in the waiting room with your mom, dad, and sister. God loves you, Greg, and He's watching out for you."

With his eyes still closed, he nodded. She squeezed his hand gently and laid it on the bed. Leaving her protective gear in the receptacle outside his cubicle, she returned to the waiting room.

The surgeon came into the waiting room to speak with Greg's parents before the surgery. Aubrey and Jeremy took Colleen with them for a late breakfast in the hospital cafeteria. Shawn insisted on giving them the money to pay for it.

On the way back, they stopped at the gift shop and let the little girl choose a small teddy bear for her brother. When Jeremy started to reach for his wallet, Aubrey laid her hand on his arm.

"Let me pay for this. We're using your car and your gas, and I want to do this for Greg."

Jeremy nodded and held Colleen's hand as Aubrey paid for the toy.

When they returned to the family lounge, a gray-jacketed volunteer led them to a waiting room outside the surgical department.

"We've been through this before." Shawn shook his head. "But it's still hard to wait." He pulled his daughter into his lap. Maureen sat beside him and rubbed his back.

"Don't feel you have to stay." Greg's mother had circles under her eyes and lines on her face. "You probably have studying to do or have other plans."

"I don't think I could leave yet." Aubrey looked at Jeremy, with his computer open, typing. "I'd rather wait until I know Greg's okay."

Jeremy looked up and nodded in agreement.

Clutching the teddy bear, Colleen fell asleep in her father's lap.

Aubrey texted Christina to fill her in on the situation, then she put her phone away. She should have remembered to bring the book she had to read for one of her classes. She sorted through the magazines in a rack on the wall of the waiting room and found one about home decorating that looked interesting, and another with pictures and articles about nature.

"Is this your last semester in college, Aubrey?" Maureen asked.

"Yes, it is."

"Do you have plans for after you graduate?" She nodded toward Jeremy.

As far as Aubrey knew, Jeremy still intended to wait. "I'm planning to get my graduate degree in Special Education. Jeremy's a first-year seminary student."

Jeremy glanced up at her and smiled when their eyes met. Did he know something she didn't?

"Greg is one of my inspirations. He worked so hard in school, and his smile made my day. I've also worked with athletes with special needs."

"I'm glad to hear that. Many people don't understand the challenges kids like Greg face, and they need good teachers."

"Greg talks about you a lot." Shawn nodded. "Thank you again for being here for him today."

After about an hour, a nurse came in. "The surgery is proceeding well, and Greg is doing fine."

Jeremy squeezed Aubrey's hand. She continued to pray.

A little later, the doctor came. Dressed in green scrubs, he walked into the lounge. "We're all done. Greg pulled through like a trouper, and in a little while you can go in to see him."

Everyone sighed, as though they'd been holding a collective breath. Tension drained out of the room.

Colleen awoke and yawned. Her father set her on the sofa and stood. Shawn shook the doctor's hand.

"Thank you, doctor." Maureen said.

Thank you, God. Aubrey returned the magazines to the rack, then went back to her seat beside Jeremy.

Jeremy finished typing, closed his laptop, and slipped it into its case. "Well, I think we should go now." Jeremy held out his hand to help Aubrey get up.

When she grasped it, a surge of electricity passed up her arm, and warmth spread through her body. He picked up her coat and held it for her as she slipped her arms into the sleeves.

"Please tell Greg we'll continue to pray for him." Aubrey tried to swallow away the lump in her throat. "May I have your address so I can write to him?"

"Of course." Shawn took a business card from his pocket and wrote on the back, then handed it to her.

"You don't know how much it means to us that you were willing to come." Maureen embraced Aubrey. "And Greg will be thrilled when he gets a letter from you."

"Greg will always be special to me." She laid one hand over her heart. "It touched my heart that he asked for me. If there's anything else I ... we can do, let me know."

Hugging the teddy bear tightly to her, Colleen put one arm around Aubrey and hugged her and then did the same to Jeremy.

Aubrey prayed for Greg and his family as she walked down the hospital corridor beside Jeremy.

2 0

hey stepped through the sliding glass doors of the hospital into a blast of cold air. Dark gray clouds filled the sky.

Thankful she'd dressed for cold weather, Aubrey shivered. Jeremy put his arm around her and pulled her close. She laid her head against his shoulder. How she loved this man!

Jeremy drove out of the hospital parking lot and headed back to campus.

"I'm glad Greg will be all right." She tugged on the cuffs of her gloves. "It meant a lot to have you there with me."

"Everyone needs help sometimes." He took a moment to gaze at her before facing the road again. "I respect your independence, but asking for help is no crime. I love you, Aubrey. I want you to ask me to help you." His declaration sent shivers through her body.

He glanced up at the sky, then turned the radio to a Christian station with music, news, and weather. The weatherman confirmed that the dark clouds overhead held snow.

Halfway back to the university, Jeremy pulled into a scenic overlook and stopped the car. "I noticed this on the way down. I thought we could stop and stretch for a few minutes."

193

"O-kay." She pulled up the zipper on her coat and followed him with her eyes as he walked around the front of the car. He had something on his mind.

He opened her door and held out his hand to help her out. His strong grip drew her up and toward him, and she raised her eyes to meet his. A thrill passed through her when she thought he might kiss her. She prepared herself.

However, he led her to a stone wall, where they could look over the snow-frosted valley below. A light snow fell in fluffy flakes around them. Embarrassed that she had misread his intentions, Aubrey took a deep breath of the cold, fresh air.

"Aubrey?"

She turned to gaze into the dark brown depths of his eyes. She loved him. She traced his face from his hairline, down his cheek, to his chin with her gloved fingers.

He smiled and placed his hands on her shoulders, then tenderly brushed strands of hair back from her face, his hand trembling. "Aubrey, I love you. Going with you today was my pleasure ... not that I wanted Greg to have to go through the accident or surgery, but because it meant we could be together helping others."

"Thank you for going with me." She rested her hands on his arms. "I'm glad you offered to pray with them. I could feel God's presence as you prayed."

"I never want to be apart from you. We belong together." He looked at her eyes, her lips, her hair, brushing at some wayward strands once again. "Will you marry me, Goldie?"

Her breath caught. She didn't expect this now. However, it took her only a few seconds to respond. "Yes, Jeremy."

"Wow!" His eyes widened. "You're sure? You don't need time to think it over?"

"Never surer." She cupped his cheek with her gloved hand and smiled. "You're the only one for me."

Stepping closer, he lowered his head. Aubrey closed her eyes.

His arms drew her closer and his lips on hers were soft and tender.

"Wow!" She giggled when he said it at the same time.

As they embraced, Jeremy whispered in Aubrey's ear. "You don't know how long I've been waiting for this opportunity, for this moment. I had almost given up hope of ever getting you to say yes, and you didn't hesitate. Willie told me to be patient, that you'd come around."

Aubrey leaned back to look into his eyes. "Should I be insulted that you talked to Willie behind my back?"

"Who knows you better than Willie?" He touched her cheek. "Your brother and I have more than one connection. He's been carrying a torch for my sister for a long time, and he's one of the most patient people I know."

"If you'd asked me last semester, I'd have said no." A sharp breath of wind chilled her. "When Leanna died, I had to make sure my life counted for something. God let me live for a reason. If I let you in, you might keep me from my goals. Mike and Willie are already on their way to success, and I didn't want to fail."

"I won't stand in your way." Jeremy grasped her shoulders. "If it's what God wants you to do, we can work this out together. We can still wait for two years, or even more if necessary, before getting married, if that's what you want."

"I know and I'm tired of fighting against how I truly feel about you. Back in the hospital, while you prayed for Greg and his family, I realized how much we could accomplish serving God together. I still believe God wants me to teach special kids, but I don't want to go through life without you."

"One night I almost lost track of why I came to Clark Seminary. I thought I might have lost you forever." He embraced her and pulled her against him. "God reminded me that when I follow and obey Him, He promised to give me my heart's desire. My heart's desire was you. Even then, however, I knew God might have something and someone different in mind for me. I had to trust Him and wait."

Enjoying the security of his arms, she closed her eyes and leaned against him. Married to Jeremy, her goals might be a little different, but together they could accomplish more.

But what about Haleigh? How would their rift affect her marriage to Jeremy?

Aubrey stepped back from him and leaned on the top of the stone wall. "What will Haleigh think of us getting married?"

The snow fell a little faster.

"I told my sister I planned to ask you." Jeremy leaned closer to her. "She's okay with it."

"She is?" She gave a nervous laugh. "Will she ever talk to me again?"

"I believe she will." Jeremy turned and gazed at the snow-veiled valley below. "I think she's almost ready to face whatever it is that made her put up a barrier to you and everything having to do with Greenlawn."

"I hope so." Aubrey shivered from the cold.

"Sometimes I think she feels the past is irredeemable, that her friends will always hold her mistakes against her." He looked around them. "I think we'd better go, Goldie. The roads will be getting slick, and we both have studying to do."

They returned to the car and its warmth, and Aubrey couldn't take her eyes off Jeremy. He smiled at her as he slid into the driver's seat and closed the door, then took off his gloves and reached into his pocket. He withdrew a small, black box and opened it to reveal a ring with a sparkling sapphire stone.

"Jeremy." She gaped. "It's gorgeous! Is that for me?" Why else would he be holding it out in front of her?

"I've been waiting to do this since last summer." He removed the ring from the box, pulled her glove from her left hand, and slipped the ring on her finger. "This was Gram's ring. I had it sized for you. If you'd rather have a different engagement ring, you don't have to accept this one."

"Oh, Jeremy, it's perfect!" Aubrey admired the ring. "And it's even more special because it was Gram's." She put her hands together under her chin. "I'll keep it!"

He leaned over. Their lips touched, and the kiss deepened. His lips against hers awakened new sensations within her. He pulled back and looked into her eyes. She took a deep breath.

"I think we'd better get going." He licked his lips. "The snow isn't letting up."

At her nod, he put his gloves on and started the car. She kept her glove off to admire her ring as Jeremy returned to the road.

As much as she wanted to hold his hand, she didn't want to distract him from his driving by touching him. He needed to concentrate on the snowy road.

She mulled over what he'd said about Haleigh. "Do you think Haleigh will agree to be a bridesmaid?"

"Thinking ahead?" He grinned. "We haven't set a date yet."

"But we will soon, right?"

"How about Valentine's Day?" He cocked his head.

"That's a month away!" She giggled.

"Well, a guy can dream, can't he?" The car slid, and he gave his full attention to driving.

Aubrey's body stiffened, and she watched the fat snowflakes falling, but her mind returned to a wedding date. "How about May, after I graduate?"

"That sounds good to me," Jeremy tensed and relaxed his fingers around the steering wheel. "But what about graduate school for you? I know you have your heart set on an advanced degree, and you've already applied. And I have another year of seminary."

"I know." She watched the windshield wipers as they rushed back and forth to clear snow from the windshield. "Everything you say is true. But do we have to wait? Maybe I can take courses online and work while you finish. I have a few years before I have to get my masters' degree for teaching." She looked at his profile. "I know you're not opposed to my plans, but somehow our plans are more important now."

The car wheels spun as they lost traction. Aubrey pressed her hand against the dashboard. "Maybe we should find a place to pull over."

"I'd rather keep going so we get back to campus sooner." Jeremy shook his head. "My car has good tires, and I'll drive carefully."

"All right." Aubrey tried to relax. Her new ring made a good distraction.

"Last summer, when Jason married Carmella, I thought he was crazy to get married before seminary," Jeremy said.

She gave him her full attention.

"I thought it would be better to wait until I finished school. Then you and I reconnected at the wedding. I've been convinced since then, at least most of the time, that we belong together. I don't want you to give up on your dreams, however. If you want to wait, we will." He shrugged. "But May sounds good to me, since you think Valentine's Day is too early."

This brought a smile to Aubrey's lips. "Let's pray about it and see what our parents think." She clasped her hands. "I'm sorry about the way I acted last semester. I felt so lonely without you, but I decided my career goals were more important."

"It's in the past. I've already forgiven you. I'm sorry I wasn't more sensitive to your needs, and that I became forgetful."

"I forgive you."

A sudden skid made Aubrey grasp the dashboard. Jeremy gripped the wheel tighter as he eased the vehicle back to a forward direction. Aubrey prayed out loud for safety.

She sighed with relief when they drove onto campus. He did the same as he pulled into the parking lot by her dorm.

"I'll be at the library after I grab a bite to eat." Aubrey drew her glove on over her left hand and lifted her purse. "Will you be coming?" She unfastened her seatbelt.

"That's the plan." He released his seatbelt and turned toward her. "Before you go, I want to ask you something else."

She held the end of the seatbelt as she waited. Her eyes met his. It was hard not to lean forward and kiss him.

"I got the internship I applied for. Will you attend Morning Star Bible Church with me, at least on Sundays?"

"If that's what you'd like." She smiled.

"It is. The semester will be getting busy, and the church expects a certain time commitment on my part. I want to take advantage of every moment we have to be together."

"I'd like that." Aubrey tipped her head. She wanted to be at his side whenever possible. "Christina and I have been substitute teachers in Sunday school for the last three years. I'll have to talk to the pastor and Sunday school superintendent first. They should know why I'm leaving Terrace Baptist."

"I agree." He laid his hand over his heart with a dramatic pose. "I can wait one more week."

"Silly," she said. She waited as he got out and opened the car door for her. Happy didn't define how she felt. Maybe ecstatic?

Inside the dormitory door, she watched as he drove away.

Christina hadn't returned yet. She called her family. They'd want to know.

"Hi, Jess ... Everything's good. Are Mom and Dad home? ... Will you put them on? ... Jess ... Yes, put it on speaker so all of you can hear ... Jess!" Aubrey shook her head as she waited for her family to gather. Just her luck to have Jesse answer the phone.

"We're all here, Aubrey," Dad said.

"Hi, Mom, Dad, Willie. I already said hi to you, Jess. I have news. Guess what? Jeremy proposed, and I said yes."

She held the phone away from her as everyone tried to talk at once. "Take it easy. You'll ruin my hearing. We visited one of my former students in the hospital this morning, and on the way back he asked me to marry him." She held up her hand and watched the facets of the sapphire catch the light.

"Congratulations, Aubrey." Dad said. "We're glad the two of you worked through your problems."

"Thank you. So am I. We want to get married in May, after I graduate. Is that all right, Mom?"

"If it's what you want. That will give us only four months, but I think we can do it."

She did a happy dance. They approved of Jeremy. She knew they would. And they agreed to the date for the wedding.

"Thanks, Mom. I'm meeting Jeremy at the library this afternoon, so I have to go. I wanted you to know right away."

Willie promised to provide the flowers, and Jesse promised to behave himself as she finished her conversation with her family.

In Aubrey's mind there remained two hurdles to overcome: the trouble with Haleigh, and the other that had been at the back of her mind since her accident as a teenager, the one Jeremy didn't know.

The following Friday afternoon, Aubrey and Jeremy prayed for good weather and headed for Greenlawn right after their classes ended. Aubrey ticked off in her mind all they had to accomplish over the weekend, including confirming the date with Pastor Pete and scheduling premarital counseling sessions.

"I've switched hours with another student. I'll have to work some of her hours next week in return for her taking my place today." Aubrey snapped her seatbelt in place.

"It gives us a little more time." Jeremy drove out of the parking lot. "We'll have to leave Greenlawn early Sunday morning to get back in time for me to meet for prayer with the other pastors." He signaled and turned onto the highway toward Greenlawn. "Our appointment with Pastor Pete is at ten o'clock tomorrow morning."

"Good." Aubrey nodded. "And Mom has made an appointment to meet with Mrs. Hayes about making my gown. I've chosen the pattern."

Jeremy grinned. "If you want my opinion, I'll be glad to give it."

Aubrey shook her head. "No, that's okay. Mom and I will take care of it." She recognized the mischievous glint in his eye.

"Do you think it's bad luck for a groom to see the dress before the wedding?"

"Of course not. It's just a fun tradition. But I want to surprise you when I walk down the aisle."

"Whatever you choose, I'm sure you'll be breathtaking."

For a few moments she dreamed about being married to this tender, considerate man, being loved and cared for by him. Sharing life with him, taking care of him. Aubrey found herself daydreaming a lot lately.

"Will you ask your brother to do the flowers?" Jeremy's voice brought her back to the present.

"Oh, Willie already volunteered. I'm excited because I know he'll do a spectacular job."

"He seems quite settled in Greenlawn. And his business is going well."

"Willie will probably succeed with anything he attempts, anywhere he decides to go. But he says God has blessed his choice to open *Floral Creations* in Greenlawn, and he's content to live there."

"And you, Aubrey?" Jeremy reached over and squeezed her hand. "Where do you want to live?"

She didn't have to think about this. "With you."

"We could end up living anywhere, even on the other side of this country, or in another country, if I'm ... we're, called to go there." He rubbed the back of her hand with his thumb. "Jason and Carmella are looking into foreign missions."

"Then we'll be called together. I can teach school almost anywhere."

All week she'd struggled to keep her mind on her classes as wedding plans spun around in her brain. As they settled some of the wedding details this weekend, she could turn her mind back to world literature, history, and missions.

"Good, we'll be Team Abbott. I don't want to go anywhere without you." He placed his hand back on the steering wheel.

For several minutes, the Christian music playing softly on the radio, the whoosh of the heater, and the click of the tires on the road filled the silence between them.

Not long ago, the possibility of them going separate ways had loomed over them.

Most couples Aubrey knew experienced conflict within their marriages, and she knew she had a lot to learn about dealing with areas where she and Jeremy disagreed. In their vows they would commit to one another "for better or for worse." Aubrey knew her independent streak could tear them apart, but she wanted to be his true partner and coworker.

Pastor Pete required premarital counseling for the couples he married. "What do you think Pastor Pete will have us do in counseling?" Aubrey asked.

"We'll talk about money and finances, the husband-wife relationship, and family, like having children and how many." He shifted his position slightly and licked his lips. "Have you thought about having a family? Do you want girls or boys, and how many?"

She watched the passing scenery, hardly seeing the snow-lined trees and drifts of snow on the fields. He didn't know about the doctor's warning that she might never be able to have children. Only she and her parents knew. "A slight possibility," the doctor had said after her accident. She'd kept the warning in the back of her mind for years. Now she had to deal with it head-on.

"I'd like to have children," she said softly. She rubbed her hand along the dashboard, finding it difficult to look directly at him.

"How many?" He looked from the road to her and back.

"Well, I'd like more than one." She pulled her ponytail to lay over her shoulder. "Katie always wanted a brother or sister. So, I think at least two. Maybe three of four." She shrugged and looked at him. "What about you?"

"I'm taking a marriage and family course this semester, and it started me thinking. I guess I always figured I'd have kids, but I never thought about it seriously." He paused and adjusted the heater dial. "Are you warm enough?"

"Yes, I'm comfortable."

"I agree with you. I'd like at least two. A boy and a girl. But I guess we'll have to be satisfied with what God gives us."

"That's true." Aubrey knew she had to tell Jeremy the truth. Was it fair to him to marry her if he really wanted children?

THEY ARRIVED in Greenlawn in time for Friday night dinner with her family, kept busy all day Saturday, and accomplished everything they planned to do. Pastor Pete gave them an outline of their counseling sessions and a list of books to read. Willie sat down with them and discussed wedding flowers. Aubrey and her mother met with the dressmaker, Mrs. Hayes, and chose the fabric for her gown.

Had it been only a week ago that Jeremy proposed?

Aubrey found a quiet moment to talk to her mother in the kitchen that evening, while Jeremy watched a basketball game on television with her father and brothers. The sounds of cheering and laughter came from the living room.

"Mom?" Aubrey sat at the kitchen table with her mother, the leftovers put away, the dishwasher whooshing and humming. Each of them sipped a cup of tea.

"Is there something on your mind, Aubrey? You look a little troubled."

"Yesterday Jeremy asked me about having ... children."

Her mother squeezed her hand. She'd heard the doctor's warning.

"I-I wasn't sure how to answer, how much to tell him."

"Don't you think he deserves the truth?"

"Of course he does. I wanted to tell him, but I couldn't. I told him I want children, and he does too. But, Mom, what if I can't have children? What will he think?"

"I think that, if he really loves you, it won't matter." Annette picked up her spoon and stirred her tea. "But I also think you have to be honest about this before you get married. If you're going to have a successful marriage, you have to learn to communicate." She looked into Aubrey's eyes. "Remember, the doctor said there was only a small chance that you couldn't have children. Don't borrow trouble."

"I know. I've known this for a long time, but it hasn't been a serious issue for me until now. I'm not sure how to tell him."

"Trust God to give you the right moment."

"What if he decides not to marry me?" She sipped her tea. A bleak thought: the future without Jeremy.

"Oh, Aubrey, *what ifs* are usually foolish. I can't predict Jeremy's reaction, but if he's the man your father and I believe he is, he's not going to let that stand in your way. You've known each other for a long time. You know his character. Trust him. But be honest with him."

Aubrey tapped her cup with her finger. Having children was an important issue for most couples she knew. Becoming Mrs. Jeremy Abbott wasn't just one of her career goals. It was her life ... their life. Jeremy had a right to know before they married.

They had to work on this together. He hadn't given up on her when she tried to cut him out of her life. She had to be honest with him and trust God for the outcome.

"Okay, Mom. I'm still not sure how to do it, but I'll try. Will you pray with me?"

"Of course, dear. It will be my pleasure." They joined hands, and her mother prayed.

"Thanks, Mom." Aubrey rinsed her empty teacup and set it in the sink. She put her arms around Mom's neck and leaned her chin on her head before she left the kitchen.

Aubrey and Jeremy finished the evening with a walk in the snow before turning in for the night. Several times, Aubrey almost brought up the subject of children, but she couldn't do it. Aubrey White, not one who usually beat around the bush on important issues, couldn't find the words to open the subject with her fiancé. *What if?* echoed in her brain.

With one last kiss, she left him at the guest room door and walked down the hall to her room.

After waking up several times during the night, she got up in the morning with a fuzzy brain, less than refreshed. She knew she'd have to tell him today, or it would gnaw at her more and more.

Dressed in her robe and slippers, Mom met them in the kitchen with two boxes of goodies to take back with them, a thermos of coffee, cinnamon rolls, and apples to eat on the way. They left before the rest of the family stirred. Streaks of daylight appeared on the horizon, and the last of the stars winked out. Aubrey shivered in the cold, and Jeremy turned up the heater.

When the car warmed up after a few minutes, Aubrey leaned her head against the seat and closed her eyes.

Jeremy told her about Morning Star Bible Church and explained some of his responsibilities. "They pay me a small salary, which helps a lot. And if I work well with them, I'll probably have the internship again next year."

"That's great." She opened her eyes and turned her head to look at him with a yawn.

"If you're tired, why don't you see if you can nap. We have a three-hour trip."

"Jeremy Abbott, what did I do to deserve such a thoughtful man as you?" She picked up his hand and brought it to her lips.

His face lit up with a smile. "You said yes to my proposal."

"You'll be okay if I fall asleep? You won't fall asleep driving?"

"I'm good." He shook his head. "I had a good night's sleep, so I'm wide awake."

Reassured, Aubrey settled back with a sigh. "Okay. I'll take a nap. But if you need me, just wake me up." She closed her eyes.

"I'll always need you, sweetheart."

"Me too," she murmured. It didn't take long for her to fall asleep.

An hour later, she opened her eyes to a bright, snow-covered landscape.

"Mornin', sunshine." Jeremy squeezed her hand. "Time to rise and shine."

"Mornin'." She smiled. "I needed that. I feel better." She sat up in her seat and stretched as much as the seatbelt allowed.

The snow sparkled in the sun's brightness. Jeremy had put on his sunglasses. The glare made Aubrey dig in her purse for hers.

"Commit your way unto the Lord," kept repeating in Aubrey's brain. She couldn't put off speaking to Jeremy about the issue that had bothered her since Friday.

She took a deep breath. "Jeremy?"

"Hmm?" His gaze rested on her for a moment before returning to the road.

"Remember in high school when I broke my hip in that accident, when Leanna died?"

"How could I forget?"

Searching for the right words, she continued. "Friday you asked me about having children."

He nodded.

"I want children. But the doctor warned me that I might not ... he said there was a slight chance I might not be able to have children." She paused, watching his profile, wishing she knew his thoughts. "I wanted you to know that."

Not looking at her right away, he passed a car and pulled back into the right-hand lane. Her stomach clenched as she waited.

"I didn't know. Is this what's been bothering you for the last couple of days?" He glanced her way and she nodded. "Thank you for telling me, Goldie."

The sound of his special name for her relieved some of the tenseness that gripped her body. She released the breath she hadn't realized she'd been holding.

He licked his lips and spoke carefully. "I'm sorry that you have had to face this uncertainty."

Their eyes met briefly.

"When you started talking about children, I didn't ..." She clasped and unclasped her hands in her lap. "I thought maybe ... wondered if it would make any difference in how you felt about marrying me. I knew I should tell you, but I ..." She twisted the ring on her finger. "My mom said that communication and honesty are necessary for a successful marriage."

"Aubrey, you know I love you?" He took a deep breath. At her nod, he continued. "I'd like to have children and be a father, but I didn't ask you to marry me just so I could have children."

He focused on the road ahead. "I want to marry you because I want to be with you, to come home to you at night, to share my life with you. I want to take care of you and love you for the rest of our lives, to grow old together. I won't say not having children won't matter, but you're most important to me."

Tears pooled in her eyes. "Thank you, Jeremy." She wiped her eyes, feeling embarrassed to cry in front of him. "I'm sorry. I don't know why, but lately I've been crying a lot."

"It's okay."

"Some girls use crying to get their own way." She shook her head. "I never want to do that to you."

"Guys often feel helpless when a woman cries. But I'll be honest, I've cried at times." He smiled at her. "Thank you, Aubrey."

"For what?"

"For trusting me enough to share something so personal. It makes me feel loved and respected by you."

A weight had been lifted from her heart and mind. "My

parents and I were the only ones who knew this. As my mother reminded me, there is only a slight chance, but it suddenly seemed like an insurmountable problem."

"I hope we'll learn to share our thoughts and problems openly. We may disagree, even have an argument or two." He winked when her eyes met his, sending a shiver to her toes. "But I never want you to be afraid to talk to me. Maybe you should make an appointment with your doctor to talk about it."

"That's probably a good idea." Aubrey sat up straighter. "I'm glad you said I shouldn't be afraid to talk to you." She pressed her thumb against her chest. "You know I'm a woman of strong opinions." She tilted her chin up.

"I know." He heaved a sigh. "I suppose I'll have to suffer through it." He joined her in laughter. "But I think the challenge will be fun." He winked at her again. Would his winks always make her feel shivery inside?

She rested her head against the back of her seat then turned to face him. "There is one other thing on my mind."

"What's that, Goldie?"

"Do you think Haleigh will agree to be a bridesmaid?"

"You'll have to ask her." He ran his fingers through his hair. "But I think she'll say yes. Our relationship has improved since Christmas. She knows we're getting married, and she told me she wants me to be happy."

"Good." Aubrey still had to work up the courage to contact Jeremy's sister. Reconciliation with Haleigh had now become a priority.

"We're almost there." Jeremy flipped his right blinker.

Aubrey tried to quell the butterflies in her stomach at the thought of attending the church as Jeremy's fiancé. She'd attended church all her life, but never as the prospective wife of a staff member. She did a lot of praying in the next few minutes.

"What do you mean, Haleigh's not here? She knew we were coming!"

Sunshine, who had greeted them with her body quivering in excitement, quickly cowered under the table.

"Calm down, Jeremy!" His mother's stern tone made Aubrey want to cower.

She bit her lip as she watched the interchange between mother and son, sharing Jeremy's disappointment at Haleigh's absence. His loud outburst had taken her by surprise and made her heart beat harder. Jeremy didn't lose his temper often.

For three weeks they'd been riding on a cloud of the newness of their engagement and the anticipation of their wedding. They'd finally come back to reality.

"I'm sorry, Mom." Jeremy brushed his hand through his hair, then reached for Aubrey's hand. "It's just that I hoped Haleigh wouldn't pull the avoidance trick again."

"Haleigh had a previous commitment at school this weekend, and she couldn't change her plans." Mrs. Abbott glanced at the clock on the wall above the sink. "Supper will be ready in about an hour. Why don't you show Aubrey her room and get settled? Your dad will be home soon."

She turned to Aubrey and smiled. "Welcome to our home, Aubrey." She held out her arms, and Aubrey stepped into them. "I want you to know I'm looking forward to having another daughter."

"Thank you." The warmth of Mrs. Abbott's embrace calmed her after Jeremy's outburst. If she could only get a similar response from Jeremy's sister.

"I'm sorry." He carried her suitcase and his up the stairs. "I expected Haleigh to be here this weekend."

"I know." She'd been rehearsing what she'd say to Haleigh.

"You'll be in Jason's old room. Mom and Dad fixed it over as a guest room."

As she followed Jeremy down the hallway, a zippered garment bag over her arm, Aubrey peeked into a distinctly feminine room. The predominance of green in its décor identified it as Haleigh's. She stopped. "Look!"

"What is it?" Jeremy asked, turning back. "Oh, that's Haleigh's room. Jason's is over here."

What had caught her eye held Aubrey's attention as she stepped into the room and walked over to the dresser. She fingered the familiar heart-shaped pendant on a chain hanging from the mirror, identical to the one in her jewelry box at home. Katie had one as well.

"Jeremy, do you know what this is?"

He set down the suitcases and entered the room. "It's a necklace Haleigh used to wear all the time. I haven't seen it for ages."

"Remember, Jeremy?" Aubrey turned and took his hands. "Haleigh bought the Three Sisters these *Best Friends Forever* necklaces for Christmas when we were in middle school."

"That's right. I remember now."

She turned again to the necklace and rubbed her finger across the inscription. And suddenly her heart filled with hope. "Jer, will you give me Haleigh's phone number?"

"You want to call her?" Jeremy laid his hands on her

shoulders and met her eyes in the mirror. "Why now? What's changed?"

"Don't you see? Haleigh still has the pendant, and she hung it on her mirror. She cares, Jeremy, and I think down deep, she wants to make things right between us. I think she'll be willing to talk to me."

"Maybe you're right." Jeremy pulled her back against him. "Maybe it's a sign." He reached over her shoulder and removed the chain from the corner of the mirror as she relaxed against his chest.

Peace washed over her, a sense that everything would be all right.

"Hmm." He laid his cheek against her hair. "I wonder if having the Three Sisters back will be safe." He smiled at her in the mirror and replaced the chain on the corner.

"I'll settle for just being friends again." Aubrey touched the pendant once more and started to pull away from him. "I guess you'd better show me the guest room."

"In a minute." Jeremy turned her to face him. He looked into her eyes, then at her lips, and lowered his to kiss her.

She closed her eyes, thrilled at the warmth of his lips against hers. Her heart thudded. "Hmm. That was nice," She laid her head against his chest, listening to his heartbeat.

A car door slammed. Sunshine yipped and whined. Aubrey stepped out of Jeremy's embrace. This time, he let her go.

"That must be Dad." Jeremy picked up the suitcases he'd set down and led the way to the guest room. He left her suitcase beside the bed. While she stepped in and looked around, Jeremy headed for his room.

A full-sized bed covered with a beige, chenille spread, a small dresser with a mirror, a straight-backed chair, and a bedside table with a lamp comprised the furnishings. The curtains at the window coordinated with the bedspread. Simple and welcoming. She hung the garment bag in the closet.

Jeremy returned, and they walked downstairs together. Sunshine met them at the bottom, her tail wagging.

"What are you, the official welcoming committee?" Aubrey sat beside Jeremy on the next-to-the-bottom step. Sunshine laid her head on Aubrey's knees, looking up at her with eyes that begged attention. She stroked the dog's head. "I'll bet you miss Haleigh when she's not here." She managed to turn her head in time to avoid a slurpy kiss from the dog.

"I'm sorry I scared you, girl." Jeremy scratched behind Sunshine's ears. The black dog turned her attention to Jeremy and licked his chin. "I guess she's forgiven me for yelling." He wiped his chin with his sleeve.

"I want to apologize for losing my temper, Aubrey." He put his arm around her shoulders and drew her against him. "I've been frustrated by my sister for so long, I just figured she'd made another excuse to avoid the issues."

She laid her hand on his. "I understand, and you're forgiven. I'll give Haleigh a call, maybe tonight or tomorrow. I have hope for a breakthrough with her. Maybe she'll at least listen and not hang up on me."

"I hope so. But I'm sorry she's not here this weekend."

"I know. Me too." Aubrey rested her head against his shoulder.

Hearing his parents' voices from the kitchen, Jeremy stood and pulled Aubrey up with him. They went to greet Jeremy's father.

"Hi, Dad." Jeremy shared a quick hug with his father.

"Good to have you home, son. The house is sometimes just too quiet." He looked at his wife, and she nodded in agreement.

"Aubrey." He turned to her with a smile. "I see my son has finally convinced you to keep him in line." He pulled her into a warm embrace. "It's good to have you in our home."

"It's nice to be here, Mr. Abbott. Thank you for your hospitality."

"Our home is always open to all our children.

Congratulations on your engagement. How are your wedding plans coming along?"

"Things are falling into place." Jeremy took Aubrey's hand and intertwined his fingers with hers. "We accomplished a lot when we were in Greenlawn." He shook his head. "I really wanted Haleigh to be home this weekend."

"I know." Jeremy's father sighed. "I'm hoping when Haleigh returns to Greenlawn for the summer, she'll be able to let go of what holds her back."

"Haleigh will definitely be going to Greenlawn this summer?" Aubrey planned to pass this information on to Willie as soon as possible.

"I believe so. She actually seems quite enthusiastic about it. The Sousas leave on sabbatical on May first, and she says she'll go after she graduates. The Sousas have given us permission to use their log home to stay in for your wedding. I think Haleigh is planning to go early and get it ready for us."

Jeremy's eyes met hers. "You're right. There is a reason to hope." She smiled and squeezed his hand.

"What can I do to help?" Aubrey turned to Jeremy's mother, who'd been listening to the conversation while she prepared the meal.

"Jeremy can show you where the dishes are, and the two of you can set the table. I'll need someone to mash potatoes and put the food into serving dishes. Then we can eat."

"That's good." Mr. Abbot kissed his wife's cheek. "I'm starved. I volunteer for potato duty."

"The food at Clark is good, as college food goes." Aubrey waited for Jeremy to hand her the plates from the cupboard. "But it's nice to have a home-cooked meal and sit down to eat as a family."

"My mouth is watering." Jeremy counted tableware from the drawer.

"Oh, yes, Jeremy and I volunteer for dish duty tonight."

Jeremy looked at her with raised eyebrows. She grinned, and he winked at her.

After the meal of oven-fried chicken, mashed potatoes, and vegetables, with chocolate pie for dessert, Aubrey washed and Jeremy dried the dishes. Aubrey lifted a handful of soapsuds and blew them at Jeremy. A brief soapsuds war erupted. The dog added her cheerful barks to their laughter.

Once they finished cleaning the kitchen, they opened their books at the kitchen table to do some reading for classes.

Afterwards Aubrey excused herself to go upstairs. "I'm going to call Haleigh," she whispered.

Jeremy joined his parents in the living room. "Aubrey has to make a phone call, then she'll be down." He sat back on the sofa.

ON HER WAY up the stairs, she heard them talking. His mother asked about their living arrangements after the wedding, and his father questioned Jeremy about the internship.

Aubrey settled against the pillows on the bed. She punched in the number Jeremy had written out for her, praying that Haleigh would talk to her. She heard three rings and expected to hear a voice mail message when Haleigh answered.

"Hello."

"Hi, Haleigh." Aubrey licked her lips. "It's nice to hear your voice." Aubrey waited for Haleigh's response. "This is Aubrey."

"I-I know. I'm just surprised you called." Haleigh sounded uncomfortable.

At least she was willing to talk. "Jeremy and I are in Wellsburg this weekend. We're sorry you're not here."

"I have a ministry assignment this weekend. I couldn't get out of it."

"Your mom told us. What do you do?"

"Once a month we do a community project. This month we have a party in a senior citizens' assisted living home."

Aubrey pulled her hair over her shoulder and wondered what to say next. "Sunshine is quite a welcoming committee. I think she misses you." Aubrey twisted her hair around her hand.

"I miss her. The senior citizens here would enjoy her." She paused. "Aubrey, congratulations on your engagement. I'm—I'm glad for you and Jeremy."

Sending up a quick thank you for what sounded like a sincere expression of sentiment, Aubrey responded. "Thank you, Haleigh. We're happy too. Will you be one of my bridesmaids?"

"I ... you want me to be a bridesmaid?"

"Of course. You're Jeremy's sister, and we're friends. Christina, my roommate, will be my maid of honor, and I've asked Carmella and Madison to be my other attendants. It wouldn't be the same without you." Aubrey held her breath as she waited for Haleigh's response.

"I'd like that."

Aubrey released her breath. "You will? Oh, good! Jeremy will be glad, and so am I. Jeremy asked Jason to be his best man, and Mike, Willie, and Jesse will be ushers."

"Did you know I'll be staying in Greenlawn for the summer? At the Sousa's."

"Your dad mentioned it." Another thought came to her mind. "I know Willie will be glad to see you."

"Yes, it has been a long time since I've been there."

Was it just the more than five years between them, or was it something else that made Jeremy's sister so hesitant to renew relationships? She searched her mind for something else to say. "Willie will be providing the wedding flowers."

"That's nice. How is his florist business doing?"

A good topic. Haleigh would talk about Willie. "It's doing well. He had a great Christmas season. It's slow this time of year though."

"That's good, I mean that his Christmas season was good."

Aubrey waited for Haleigh to say more. She didn't, but at least she didn't hang up.

"I'll have my mother send the pattern and fabric for a bridesmaid's dress here, if you're willing to sew your own dress."

"I can sew my dress. I think I'll have time on spring break. Thank you, Aubrey, for asking me." Was that a smile in Haleigh's voice? "I assume the color will be blue."

"Of course. What other color is there?" She expected Haleigh to say green. "I saw the pendant on your mirror. I still have mine too."

"Yes. I found it during Christmas break." Haleigh sighed. "It brought back memories."

"Good ones, I hope." Aubrey didn't wait for a response to her comment. "I guess I'd better get back downstairs. I'm glad you'll be in the wedding. We'll have to get together sometime."

"Okay. Please give my love to my family."

"Yes, I'll do that." After she talked to Jeremy. "Bye, Haleigh."

"Bye."

Aubrey took a deep breath and blew it out as she clicked off her phone. Although not the most comfortable conversation she'd ever had, another hurdle had been jumped, clearing the path to their wedding. She hoped Haleigh understood she wanted to renew their friendship because she wanted them to be friends, not just because she was marrying her brother.

At the base of the stairs, she caught Jeremy's eye and nodded. He patted the sofa. She sat next to him and leaned against him. He rested his arm behind her on the sofa.

"I was wondering." Jeremy's father said. "Will you young people walk the dog tonight and let these old people stay inside where it's warm?"

Aubrey didn't consider Jeremy's parents, or her own, old. Sunshine, lying curled up on the floor beside his chair, wagged her tail at the word *walk*.

"We surely will, won't we, honey?" Jeremy stood and pulled Aubrey to her feet.

"I haven't had a run today." Aubrey stretched and rubbed her hip. "I think I need to move a bit." And talk to Jeremy in private.

Sunshine stood, yawned, and walked over to them.

"She understands the word *walk*, and she loves them." Mrs. Abbott went into the kitchen and returned with the dog's leash. "When Haleigh isn't home, we take her out, but I'd be glad to have you do it tonight."

"What do you think, Sunshine?" Jeremy scratched the dog behind her ear.

Woof! The dog pranced around and wagged her tail furiously. *Woof!*

"I think she agrees. Haleigh has done such a good job training her." Aubrey compared the cute, black puppy she remembered to the happy, mature dog before her.

"We all laughed when Haleigh named her Sunshine." The dog looked at Mr. Abbott when he said her name. "But she's given all of us so much happiness. Haleigh especially. She's a happy dog, and she knows how to make anyone feel better. We're proud of what Haleigh has accomplished with her as a therapy dog."

"Mike's wife, Madison, has a therapy dog. His name is Hammurabi. She said it's because he was such a rambunctious puppy, and the name is exotic." Aubrey stroked Sunshine's back.

"Therapy dogs have to be well trained to obey commands and to be quiet around sick people," Mr. Abbott said. "I've seen times when Haleigh is upset, and Sunshine knows just how to help her. I'm so grateful my mother knew a dog would be good for Haleigh."

"I have many good memories of Gram." Aubrey twisted the ring on her finger. "I think of her when I see a flower garden or the constellations. I think all of us thought of her as our grandmother."

With tears in his eyes, Mr. Abbot smiled.

Aubrey and Jeremy put on their boots, coats, hats, and gloves, and wrapped scarves around their necks. Jeremy snapped

Sunshine's leash to her collar, and they went out the door. With her nose in the snow, Sunshine pranced and snuffled.

Their breath formed mist in the cold night air. Stars twinkled overhead in the darkness, and the Milky Way made a shining path across the sky. Aubrey clasped Jeremy's left hand as he held Sunshine's leash with his right. They walked at a brisk pace, the dog trotting beside them.

"So, tell me about your call to Haleigh. I take it she talked to you." Sunshine looked at him when he said his sister's name.

"Yes, she did." Aubrey blew out a breath, watching the fog disperse. "God answered that prayer. But I could tell she wasn't comfortable."

"What did she say?"

"Well, she seemed surprised that I'd ask her to be a bridesmaid, but she said yes and that she'd make her dress."

"Good."

"Actually, she congratulated us on our engagement, and I think she meant it."

The drone of an airplane flying overhead broke into the evening quiet around them. When a neighbor's dog barked, Sunshine pricked up her ears with a muffled woof.

"It's okay, girl." Jeremy patted her head. Sunshine wagged her tail and continued walking.

Jeremy let go of Aubrey's hand and put his arm around her shoulders. "I hoped she'd be okay with it. She told me she would."

"I feel like we've jumped another hurdle. We have our wedding party now, and our plans are in motion for May. But I've got another problem."

"What's the matter?"

"I'm finding it hard to concentrate on my classes. I think I'm falling behind."

The only time Aubrey had fallen behind in her schoolwork was after her high school accident, but with the help of a tutor she'd caught up and finished the school year. They walked in silence for a short distance.

So far this semester she'd done all her reading, had handed in papers on time, and had passed her tests. No, she hadn't fallen behind yet. But keeping her mind on her studies proved difficult.

"I know what you mean." Jeremy took her hand again. "I'm finding it hard, too, along with the internship. We'll work this out together. Except for counselling sessions with Pastor Pete, we won't be traveling again until spring break, and we've accomplished so much in a short time for our wedding. Our moms will put together all the details for the reception, and they've both said they'd help in any way we needed them.

"You're right."

"We'll have to make sure we concentrate on our studies and help each other get through." He squeezed her hand. "We want to honor God in everything we do."

"Look, Jer, a shooting star!"

They both watched the streak of light in the brief moment before it winked out. She stopped and faced him. The dog looked at them, then sat and waited quietly beside Jeremy.

"You know, what I see as a hurdle to my goals, you see as an opportunity to find a solution. I love you, Jeremy Abbott. I don't think I deserve such a special man, especially after the way I treated you."

He brushed her face with a gloved hand and tenderly kissed her. For a moment she forgot the cold and the dog. The kiss ended when a car turned the corner, its headlights bright as it approached. She stepped back to his side, and they continued to walk.

"You're the love of my life, Aubrey White. I look forward to being together with you for the rest of our lives. We both have a lot to learn, especially about forgiveness and finding solutions. But we belong together."

"Like bread and butter," Aubrey said.

"Like horse and carriage," Jeremy added.

"Like sugar and spice."

"Like the moon and stars."

"Like paper and pen."

"Like cinnamon and toast."

"Like coffee and cream."

"Like ... like ..." Jeremy couldn't think of another simile.

And neither could she. They both broke down laughing. Sunshine joined their laughter with a short bark.

They returned to the house, their noses and cheeks red and their fingers and toes numb. Jeremy offered to make hot chocolate.

"With marshmallows?"

He raised his eyebrows. "What other way is there?"

At the kitchen table, Aubrey sat beside him. They each had a steaming mug of hot chocolate topped with marshmallows before them. Sunshine curled up under the table at their feet.

"If we spend tomorrow morning studying, we'll have time to take a walk and have some fun in the afternoon." Sunshine's tail thumped on the floor. Jeremy peered under the table. "I think she heard me say *walk*."

"I think she's laughing at us." Aubrey pushed her chair out so she could see Sunshine. Resting her muzzle on her front paws, Sunshine looked up at her. "I can see a twinkle in her eyes." The dog's tail thumped again.

"Probably."

Aubrey looked up to find Jeremy watching her. She blew him a kiss.

"I think she's adopted us while we're here." He blew one back.

"At least Haleigh will be able to take her dog with her this summer." Aubrey straightened in her chair. "I wonder if Sunshine will remember Greenlawn." She sipped from her mug.

"You have a marshmallow mustache, Goldie."

She licked it off and took another sip, aware that he watched her over the top of his mug.

"I'm sure Haleigh's dog will be happy to be with my sister wherever she goes."

"I think so." Aubrey sighed and leaned back in her chair, then reached for his hand and clasped it. "I'm glad we have this weekend together with your mom and dad. I don't think I've relaxed this much since my days off during the summer.

"When I think how I complained when we didn't have more time last semester, and then I nearly gave up on us ..." She shook her head. "I would have missed out on all this. When we wait for God's time and place, we're blessed."

Jeremy cupped her jaw with his hand, gently rubbing her cheek with his thumb. "One night I became discouraged, and God reminded me of a verse from Psalm 37: 'Commit your way to the Lord, Trust also in Him, And He shall bring it to pass.' That's verse five." He dropped his hand from her jaw and clasped her hand between both of his.

"That verse is imprinted on my brain and my heart. That promise from God, and Willie's encouragement not to give up on you, kept me believing you and I would one day be together."

Aubrey looked deeply into Jeremy's dark brown eyes as they leaned toward each other. Their lips met.

"Pastor Pete asked us whether we want to write our own vows or use traditional ones. What do you think, Goldie?"

"I think I'd like to marry you." She tipped her head.

"That's good, since we're planning our wedding." He laughed. "But what about the vows?"

"I'd like for us to try to write our own." She held both his hands in hers. "I like the traditional ones, but I want ours to be special, just for us."

"As long as you promise to love me forever."

"Woof!" agreed Sunshine from her dreams at their feet.

ABOUT THE AUTHOR

Beth's first published work, a poem about her lamb that she wrote in second grade, appeared in the school newspaper. She also wrote puppet plays that she and her brother performed for school talent shows. She later wrote ventriloquist routines for her husband to perform with his dummies

Beth grew up in a rural, Upstate New York community, the youngest of seven children. After graduating from Hartwick College in Oneonta, NY, she married Frank. They raised three children and now have five granddaughters. She enjoys reading, gardening and sewing.

For more than thirty years, Beth worked alongside Frank in Christian ministry, first with Child Evangelism Fellowship and then in pastoral ministry in several churches. She taught Bible classes to children, teens, and women. As well as teaching, Beth was involved in church music ministry.

A 4-H member for nine years, she became a 4-H leader when

her children belonged to 4-H. She home schooled her children for twelve years.

A life-long lover of books and reading, Beth's first Christian romance novel, *Meadow Song,* debuted in 2018. Lillenas Drama accepted some of her church holiday manuscripts for publication in their Christmas, Easter, and Thanksgiving *Program Builders.* Several devotions appeared in *Penned for the Heart* and one in *The Secret Place.* Her short story "Sadie and the Princess" is included in *Heart-warming Horse Stories* on Amazon.

Meadow Song

Artist Kate Greenway escapes her home town after the death of her finance. She finds a meadow to paint in, a young girl, and the girl's handsome uncle Jack Chambers and begins to move forward in her life. When Kate's mother develops cancer, Kate has to return home to care for her. Jack cannot make a commitment. She tells Jack the Master Potter can create something new out of the broken pieces of their lives.

Cake That! by Heather Greer

Ten bakers. Nine days. One winner.

Competing on the *Cake That* baking show is a dream come true for
Livvy Miller, but debt on her cupcake truck and an expensive repair
make her question if it's one she should chase. Her best friend, Tabitha,
encourages Livvy to trust God to care for The Sugar Cube, win or lose.

Family is everything to Evan Jones. His parents always gave up their
dreams so their children could achieve theirs. Winning *Cake That* would
let him give back some of what they've sacrificed by allowing him to
give them the trip they've always talked about but could never afford.

As the contestants live and bake together, more than the competition heats up. Livvy and Evan have a spark from the start, but they're in it to win. Neither needs the distraction of romance. Unwanted attention from Will, another competitor, complicates matters. Stir in strange occurrences to the daily baking assignments, and everyone wonders if a saboteur is in the mix.

With the distractions inside and outside the *Cake That* kitchen, will Livvy or Evan rise above the rest and claim the prize? Or does God have more in store for them than they first imagined?

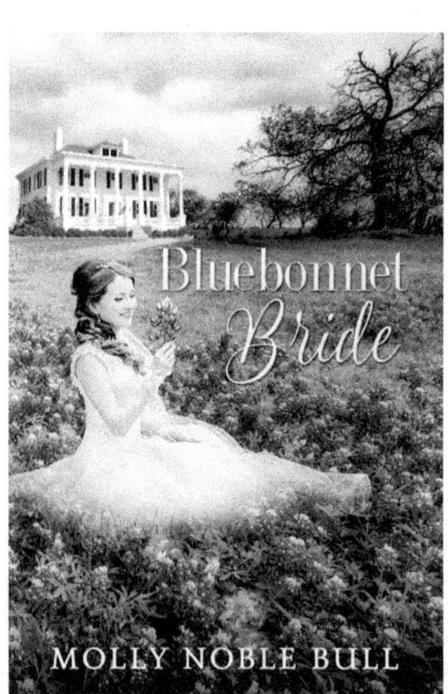

Bluebonnet Bride by Molly Noble Bull

Gina Hollister, a dyslexic with a PhD in educational psychology, is hired by widower and business tycoon, Steve Bryson, to tutor his fourteen-year-old daughter for the summer at his Durango, Colorado, mansion that Gina calls a castle.

An attraction soon develops between Gina and Steve. However, their romance can never end in marriage because Gina believes the lies about

Steve's womanizing, and he claims he'll never marry again—even to a beautiful Bible Thumper like Dr. Gina Hollister.

Saving Grace by Amy Anguish

Michelle Wilson's one goal in life was to become a top journalist at the local paper back in her hometown of Cedar Springs, AR. But on the way to bringing that dream to reality, a life-changing wreck interrupts Michelle's plans and adds an orphaned baby into the mix. Now, she has tough decisions ahead—did God put her in that accident to save baby Grace? And if so, why is it so hard to convince everyone else she should be the baby's new mommy?

Greg Marshall has been Michelle's best friend his whole life. He's thrilled she's moving back home, but not so sure about her sudden desire to be a single mom. His feelings for her have grown through the years, but she's never seemed to notice. Can he help Michelle with the adoption and grow their relationship at the same time?

Forever Music by Hope Toler Dougherty

A battered heart needs healing.

A community needs rescuing.

A chartered course needs redirecting.

College history instructor, Josie Daniels is good at mothering her three brothers, volunteering in her community, and getting over broken hearts, but meeting aloof, hotshot attorney Ches Windham challenges her nurturing, positive-thinking spirit.

Josie longs to help Ches find his true purpose, but as his hidden talents and true personality emerge. Will she be able to withstand his potent charms, or will she lose her heart in the process?

A rising star in his law firm, Ches Windham is good at keeping secrets.

He's always been the good son, following his father's will to become an attorney and playing the game for a fast track to partnering with a law firm. Lately, though his life's path has lost whatever luster it had—all because of his unlikely, and unacceptable, friendship with Josie. He struggles between the life he's prepared for and the one calling to him now. Opposing his father has never been an option, and spending time with Josie can't be one. The more he's with her, however, the more he wants to be.

When a crisis tarnishes his golden future and secrets are revealed, Ches is forced to reexamine the trajectory of his life. Will he choose the path his father hammered out for him or the path that speaks to his heart?

www.ingramcontent.com/pod-product-compliance
Lightning Source LLC
Chambersburg PA
CBHW070640100726